Earwig

Also by B. Catling

The Vorrh
The Erstwhile
The Cloven

Earwig

B. Catling

CORONET

First published in Great Britain in 2019 by Coronet
An Imprint of Hodder & Stoughton
An Hachette UK company

1

Copyright © B. Catling 2019

The right of Brian Catling to be identified as the Author of the Work has been asserted by him in accordance with the Copyright, Designs and Patents Act 1988.

A CIP catalogue record for this title is available from the British Library

Hardback ISBN 978 1 473 68710 3
Trade Paperback ISBN 978 1 473 68711 0
eBook ISBN 978 1 473 68713 4

Typeset in Minion Pro by Hewer Text UK Ltd, Edinburgh
Printed and bound in Great Britain by Clays Ltd, Elcograf S.p.A.

Hodder & Stoughton policy is to use papers that are natural, renewable and recyclable products and made from wood grown in sustainable forests. The logging and manufacturing processes are expected to conform to the environmental regulations of the country of origin.

Hodder & Stoughton Ltd
Carmelite House
50 Victoria Embankment
London EC4Y 0DZ

www.hodder.co.uk

To my nippers: Jack, Flossie and Finn

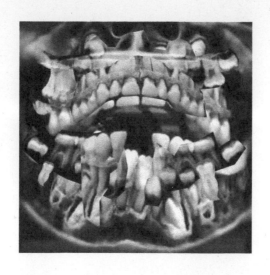

One

BROWN

*I*t was long and thin; its outer casing was dark brown, jointed about its neck, thorax, abdomen and lower waist. It was dry as a small desert's wind and moved its limbs in a long, spiky manner without the slightest display of energy or commitment to action. The head looked entirely bald, but was in fact shaded by long strands of colourless hair that were swept back to an oily ridge at its back. The eyes were wide apart and heavily lidded with a dull expression. The ears and the polished shoes were the most remarkable features. Both had been fastidiously preened. Long tufts of yellowish hair sprouted from the ear's thin helices and were drawn upwards to extend their length and in some species of sunlight appeared equally translucent, like antennae of tight amber. The shoes seemed far too long; reminiscent of the famous 'big boots' worn by the diminutive music hall star Little Titch. Except they were not straight and scuffed, but immaculate and curiously turned inwards in a way that suggested a scimitar. Their hard, light brown surfaces glistened like horn as they dangled under the shadow of the circular walnut table.

It was in the kitchen nibbling at the crumbs of bread that surrounded a half-filled bowl of brown bitter coffee.

Its name was Herr Aalbert Scellinc.

The slender glass tube that curled down little Mia's chin had been fashioned by a jeweller who had been a glass blower employed to shape intricate vessels and air-thin complex tubes and pipettes in a department of organic chemistry, belonging to the great University of Leiden. She wore it all her waking hours, only removing it for eating and sleep.

Mia kept every possible drop of her saliva so that she could make more transitory teeth for her tiny, insatiable mouth. The original ones had all been removed early in her life, each tooth lovingly cleaned so that a fine plaster mould could be made from its unique shape and size. Then a series of rubber, watertight moulds had been made from the first impression; hundreds of them, so that they would never wear out and would always be there. Identical. She would decant her saliva into their delicate hollows three times a day, and place the rubbers on a green glass tray, which she slid into the freezing compartment of her humming refrigerator.

The new teeth of her own frozen spit would be ready and waiting to be fitted into her gums in three hours. Or a little longer in the summer time, when the old paraffin-powered heart of the machine found it more difficult to pump icy fluids around its juddering copper pipes.

Her gums had been surgically prepared to receive the constant changing harvest of restless ice. Minor readjustments were made as she grew. Fortunately her body never grew very much in those early years, so the operations were small and generally only conducted with a local anaesthetic, and sometimes with none at all. Because, in truth, Mia had come to like the sharp jolts of gleaming instruments and to savour the colours of gnawing aches. The mouth surgeon was the only person ever allowed into the tightly locked apartment.

Mia lived with Herr Aalbert, in a spacious and high-ceilinged apartment on the third floor of a grand house, part of a long row that graced one of the wider boulevards of the city of Liège.

The sound of the refrigerator echoed far out of its corner in the pristine kitchen. It was a solid upright wooden cabinet fringed and buckled with sturdy brass hinges and latching handles. It was the darkest thing in the room and indeed in the entire apartment. Its phases of gentle rumbling filled the glass and mirrored interiors of the six interconnecting rooms with an almost human and melodic warmth, unlike its predecessor that had taken up a room of its own and sounded like the furious crescendos of a hen coop competing with the gritty bass tones of a steamroller. Ferdinand Carré's device had not been built for a domestic home. His machine for making ice was meant to stretch its pipes, boilers and ventricles in cargo ships, and was never intended to splutter near the gentility of a growing young woman.

The new cold box had been severely modified to ensure that deep permafrost existed in each little tooth. The ice core was hard as steel, which meant that each tooth had a likely life of at least two hours or more depending on how inquisitive Mia's tongue had been since its implanting. The new refrigerator and the new hardness of the teeth delighted Mia, who spent a considerable part of her life in relationship with it. But Herr Aalbert despised it, and shuddered each time it murmured, because it confused and distorted the audible contours of this flat he was paid to live in. He listened intently trying to understand the space around him. He had trained himself from childhood to know where everybody was and who might be approaching and who might be hurting somebody else. If he chose to, he could precisely locate the exact place in a distant room where a mouse was scratching. Or know on what floor a tap was dripping. Or locate the chimney and fireplace that encouraged the wind to moan there. The previous ice machine's noise had been contained, locked up in its own room. The new machine had been made to share his habitat and voice out through open doors and corridors at will. Again its sound flooded out from the kitchen through all the rooms and he hissed '*Doodskist*' under his hard thin breath.

The great city of Liège bulges under the Netherlands and the weight of Germany to its east. But its knotted spine is pure Ardennes; a city of guns and garlic that speaks its Walloon, German and French through barriers of a gentle mutual contempt. Herr Aalbert's parents had both been German, but he was fiercely Dutch and chose to speak in that tongue, with occasional flurries of French or English, most of which were reserved for matters of food and drink in the former and foul cursing in the latter. Aalbert's father had spent time imprisoned in England and the tough old man spat out Anglo-Saxon abuse with great relish. In fact by the age of six Aalbert had been fluent in three tongues-worth of expletives. When away from respectable company, or those he was forced to 'respect', he frequently launched into roared long sessions of meaningless swearing, like a valve letting off the frustrations and torments that come from a hypocritical subservience, manifest in both his fastidious care for Mia's life and the sly ways he listened in on it. Drinking glasses of different shapes and sizes were placed in the rooms next to her bedroom and adjoining bathroom. Three for her sleeping and dressing. Four for her naked toilet, some so delicate that he could hear the curve and anxiety of her growing adolescence within the precision of one waxy ear.

Herr Aalbert had never touched her and never intended to. He had been employed to wash, clean, cook and to never let Mia leave the confines of the six rooms. He reported weekly by telephone on the child's health and well-being. He undertook his duties and obligation with diligence and a bony, humourless vigour. She was 'safe' in his care and he classified his listening as little more than a personal bonus, an extra observation that was well earned and caused no harm, as long as it remained secret.

Herr Aalbert had been living with the child for the last three years, during which she had hardly ever spoken to him. Mia was self-possessed and indifferent to his attentions and he had long since shelved the little curiosity he had about her origins or identity, such speculations not being part of his job. He knew that she was not a mute because he had heard her talking to her teeth in a mumbled gummy voice that was surprisingly deep for one so small, sometimes in her bedroom and sometimes standing next to the freezing machine. But mostly he heard her through the glass that he held against the various walls of the apartments. There was something about the disengaged sound, the voice inside the wrong space, that gave him subdued pleasure.

The truth was that he had never really trusted his eyes. He knew they played tricks. His mother had convinced him that he had not seen any of the brutal things his father had done. This had crippled his visual memory and stunted all imagination attached to sight. But meanwhile his hearing stayed intact and grew in seclusion, making a nest of remembrance from twisted sticks of shouts, twigs of cries and feathers of sobs. He trusted his listening and it had protected him and gifted him a concealed power.

It had been his astute sense of hearing that had kept him alive in the mud of the Great War. Indeed it had been responsible for placing him on much drier land in 1917.

His 'gift' had been discovered when a military field experiment had been seeking 'volunteers' for a special unit testing acoustic sensing devices, a pre-radar means of identifying approaching planes or airships. These primitive listening tools were two huge trumpets of metal; cones pointing wide-end upwards into the clouds and rain. From the thin tapering end ran a tube into the ears of the operator, who would swivel the device while searching the skies.

There were many different prototypes tested, the most bizarre being a captured German headset that was comprised of two front-facing horns attached to a mask made of leather and rubber. Strong optical lenses, calibrated to infinity, were set into the goggle section. Aalbert and eight other men would stand in a curved row, slowly turning their heads to collect the sound of an engine chewing the clouds at some distant point. The lenses would then help them pinpoint the target for the banks of anti-aircraft guns. He would spend hours wearing this technical gargoyle, moving like a dummy or an insect. He had no doubt that this odd assignment and these impossible inventions had saved his life. So the ticks and stiffness they had instilled in him were a small price to pay.

Eventually he was assigned to a lone hillock beyond the range of rifle fire and outside of artillery bombardment; there he would listen for hours on end. The uncanny amplification of the waste-land and its mournful skies channelled directly into his brain. He had learnt to unhook most of his thinking while he endured these listening duties, and found something like solace in the grey swivelling landscape between his ears. It was during these moments of concentration and expectation that he had learnt to focus ten per cent of his awareness elsewhere, to separate a small section of alertness for emergencies.

He and two other listeners were stationed at the rim of no man's land, each attached to their own set of enormous trumpets. They looked out over the banks of a flooded and cratered river and listened through all the water for the drone of incoming enemies.

For some reason nobody could explain, one of the distant pieces of long range artillery must have swivelled around to fire one, meaningless round in their direction. Aalbert had heard its approaching whistle long before the other two men had heard the distant report. He snatched the tubes out of his ears and ducked down, covering his head. The shell exploded at a safe distance, five hundred metres from where they were installed. After the explosion he got up and brushed the loose mud off his trench coat, turning towards his comrades. One was still standing, the other lay face down in the drying mud; both were still connected to their cones. He cautiously walked closer to the standing man and, as his face came into sight, heard a trickle.

Aalbert stopped rigid when he saw the standing man was dead. Blood was pulsing out of the empty eye sockets of his white face. When Aalbert was capable of dragging his attention away, he went to the other man and turned his stiff body over. The same terrible injury had occurred. They had both been shot, inside out, the terrible volume of the explosion rifling through their heads and finding the softest, least resistant exit.

He had continued to man his post for three days until a relief party arrived, some of whom said they were disgusted that he had not covered the wrecked faces of his comrades.

He had been concerned instead with becoming even more cautious and attentive to sounds from afar, and this had made him strain his hearing deeper into the apparatus.

But it had been on last day of that solitary post that he heard something that devastated his life and convalesced him out of the war. He had been standing on the familiar high ground, pointing his array of cones out over the black stumps of tortured woodland. The birds were gone so there was no interference in the tubes other than the mournful wind and the constant rumble behind him of distant guns. Then the scratched voice came to him as sharp as a gramophone needle inscribing into the bone of his skull. It sounded like his father; the same London inflection and guttural tone of accusation. Just one word, gnarled under his breath, the same word he had branded the young Aalbert with when he caught him hovering near doors and sipping at conversations he could never understand.

One word: Earwig.

Aalbert had learnt to listen to movements, especially the old man's. Aalbert was capable of predicting his changes of mood in advance of them occurring. He heard minute changes of posture and breath and their infliction into the furniture and floorboards. The quietness of growing irritation, the splintering of simmering anger and the inevitable screaming hurtle into rage. The army had been a blessing, an escape from the tyranny and depression of his home, and he had never returned even after he was released from military service and medical rehabilitation.

Like so many of the wounded, aimless and disappointed, he drifted after the war was over, wanting to distance himself from the killing grounds of northern France. For a while he found work on the grit and aggregate barges that plied the great Maas, mainly as the nightwatchman, keeping guard while the rest of the crew were sleeping or roistering in the town that clung to the river's banks. Something about the endlessness of the water and quietness of drifting with tons of floating stone gave him the sense of distance that he needed. But the work was part-time and he often found himself between jobs stranded in the countryside at the water's edge.

He finally stepped off the boats in Limburg and found shabby employment in the towns and cities of that domain. At the age of fifty-one Herr Aalbert had been a kitchen assistant, a male nurse and a nightwatchman – before securing the present comfort of his position with Mia.

The job in the advert that he applied for had nothing to do with the one he was eventually given. He often wondered why such an elaborate ruse had been necessary and also wondered why he had been chosen over the other applicants. He knew he was a man of original and defined talents, but nobody else had ever seen them, ever. His speculation on this was a narrow thing and without any sustained enquiry.

'Caretaker Required', the advert said. 'Foreign owners require a trustworthy person to be responsible for the upkeep of a grand apartment in central Liège for a minimum of three to a maximum of five years. The successful applicant is expected to live alone and not allow access to any other person without previous permission of the owners. One of the rooms in the apartment is also occupied.' Aalbert read this in a newspaper in Au Metro, a bar that he frequented twice a week when he could afford it, preferring early weekday mornings when the place was almost empty. On that day slanted sunlight warmed the dull hum of its emptiness, chaffing the last night's smell of drink and tobacco. He made his application there and then asking Gervas the owner for a pencil and paper.

The interview was held six weeks later in Maastricht, the Catholic Church's strongest foothold in protestant Holland. The address was impressive, being in the *Vrijthof*, the ancient city's central square in the shadow of the Basilica of Saint Servatius. He approached a three-storey, quietly imposing house, with its door open onto the activity of a bright morning. Aalbert read the letter again and started to climb the weary creaking wooden stairs, the sounds of the world outside dispersing. The office was on the top floor, tiny and unnamed. The landing outside was dim and silent; the only illumination he could discover was coming from a small skylight. He knocked on the door with a poorly stencilled number 10 on its frosted glass, which rattled in its putty. Nobody answered. He stepped back and waited. Then, taking the letter out again, he held it up towards the skylight to read. This was certainly the place. He then tried the brass door knob. It was locked. He turned back towards the dark stairs when a bell rang, sharp and pointed in a resonance that stung his inner ear.

Aalbert had a problem with bells. Over the years they had become attached to some of his most distressing memories, which he had long since buried. Their insistent sound made his deep anxieties turn in their shallow graves. He waited for the sound to fade and then returned to the door and twisted the knob again. This time it opened and the surprise of this did not give him time to marvel at how it could have occurred.

He looked through the empty first room into another and saw a table with a woman sitting behind it. She was wearing a dark blue dress and her beautiful feet were shoeless and not quite touching the polished wooden floor, which caught the sheen of her painted vermilion toenails. Her head and shoulders were in shadow.

The blur of her hand moved over the table and the bell needled his ear again. It partially exhumed a recollection of another woman in another time. He felt himself totter in a nervous daze, his suddenly unfocused body pinched in the freshly starched shirt and sagging-in trousers that were two sizes too large. The name of this woman of long ago had been Maria and he had shared the only intimate moment of his life with her. But her family had ended all the beginnings of any future they might have had, and he had run away, alarm bells ringing as the house where they had been hiding burst into flames.

He teetered forward and stood before the table. The dim light in the room was clinging to the brass service bell. The woman's face was still in shadow. Then she spoke in a voice he would never forget: 'Is it too dark for you here?'

The voice was a purr rising up through a lift shaft of oiled wires; it instantly removed the spite of the bell.

'Would you prefer the blinds open?'

Aalbert was seeking words to reply with when her hand, immaculately manicured with the same vermilion varnish, pointed sideways.

'Please try.'

One finger, he saw, was pointing at a steel handle held in a bracket next to a sealed window frame. Still in a dream he stepped up to the contrivance and attempted to turn it.

It did not move. He held it tight and still with one hand while feeling around and behind its contours, seeking a tell to its mechanical design. He was about to let go when he felt a movement in its axis. He pushed against it and wrenched the handle, letting in blinding sunlight.

'All the way,' she said, and so he cranked it and the shutters on the other side of the window glass wrenched wide open. The window was behind the woman and now he was unable to see her in the brilliance burning in through the dusty glass. The light devoured the shadows that had previously mantled her head in a way that made her twice as invisible.

'You are a clever man. I can see that Scellinc. I have only three questions for you?'

Aalbert's eyes were watering and his collar was razoring his sweating neck.

'Do you have a partner or a family?'

'No.'

'Can you be trusted to do exactly what you are told?'

'Yes.'

'If the fee mentioned for this position was doubled, could you be trusted twice as much?'

'But there was no fee mentioned.'

'Then name one.'

Aalbert did.

'Now double it.'

He was flabbergasted.

'Are you afraid of children?' she said.

'That's a fourth question,' he mumbled boldly, still in a delirium because of the money proposed.

'There is always another question, you know that.'

His employer had only told him the details about caring for the child some weeks later, after they paid him a large advance and he had signed all the pages of the complex contract. He then thought about arguing or even running away. But there was no way out. Soon he had spent a considerable amount of the advance and had no way of paying it back. He also recognised that he worked for very powerful people – and all the other conditions of this job suited him perfectly. So began the routine of their imprisoned days. Over the years the routine became woven tighter into what only he could ever consider to be normal. Nobody but the specialist doctor ever got past the front door. All their needs were brought to that portal and he hardly ever went out. Aalbert liked the seclusion and ran the apartment and his life with stern resolve.

He held the heavy telephone receiver close to his head and was enjoying the taste of it and the odour of his breath as it reflected back from the mouthpiece. It was 7 p.m. on another Friday night – his appointed time to report to his employers, whom he vaguely assumed to be the child's guardians. The brief conversation was always the same. So he nearly dropped the telephone when the other speaker announced that the child was 'to be made ready to leave' during the next week and that he was expected to escort her across Belgium to Paris. After the call he still held the empty mouthpiece close to his face, ignoring the drone that said the other speaker had hung up. He stood in shock, his gaunt frame leaning against the faded rococo plasterwork near the door. His other hand held the stub of a pencil that hung from the string of the notepad fixed to the wall next to the telephone.

One scrawled word was on the pad, a word he had vaguely heard before, thinly attached to the smell of fireworks, damp nights and gardens. He had never expected such a task to be given to him, never expected to leave what had become his most permanent dwelling. All kinds of forgotten fears crept out of hiding from the few folds in his underused brain. Fears of his responsibility being tested, gauged against the complexities of the outside world. Fears of failure and mockery, and worst of all the fear of being found out. What might the child say about him if she met other people? And would they visit the apartment in his absence and pry? He must remember to remove all the glasses before they left. The thought of the glasses made him aware of the receiver in his clammy hand, which was shuddering with anxiety. He hung up the phone and shuffled to his bedroom and found the cognac, swallowing a large cupful before sitting on the bed. He poured another. Maybe it would not be so bad? They had not said the train went all the way without the need to change, and surely they would be travelling first class? He caught sight of his thin face, like a worn-out albino slipper hanging in the shadowy bruise of the wardrobe mirror. The refrigerator awoke and rumbled the sharpness in the glass into a blur. Aalbert poured another drink. How would he stop her running away, either from fear or the glamour of the wide outside world? Perhaps a leash, he thought – the kind of rein that was normal to attach to much younger children – and then he reconsidered. No, that would cause too much comment on an adolescent. It might arouse suspicion in the eyes of the authorities. Perhaps he might subdue her with drink or some of the sleeping linctus that he took every night. He became despondent at the idea of putting her drooling little body into abeyance, pulling it through Europe in the closed compartment of the train. He drank again and the warming fluid gave him hope. Practice, that was it. Practice would make all perfect. Practice here in his city, which he knew like the back of his hand. Do it first among those who knew him and those who might help if he practised taking her outside in small stages. The idea seemed to be brilliant, warmed by the alcohol.

The next morning the sun felt unnecessarily bright. It blinded all the glass and white paint in the apartment as Herr Aalbert skulked in the corridor for as long as possible. Outside it was duller; he had extra shopping to do that day and did not savour the prospect. He had never bought clothing for anybody else before and the idea of buying a topcoat and some sturdy shoes for Mia filled him with trepidation.

Madame Oiswennier's *parlour de dame* had never entertained a customer like the Earwig.

Madame was a large woman with rose-coloured (and scented) hair. She was strict, courteous and aloof and tried not to glare at Aalbert as he dithered between extremes; a loud, chequered jacket of a thick woollen weave and a slender, drab cape.

He was weighing up the value of dressing Mia bright enough so that he might see her if she ran away or dull enough that she would not attract the attention of strangers. Such extremes of odd and vulgar preference had never been considered in Madame Oiswennier's parlour before. Not that Aalbert spoke a word of his dilemma to the formidable lady, but she could divine his quandary in the winces and pale gulpings of what he considered his poker face. She turned away to give him a moment to finger the garments a little more. He did so and decided on the cape.

The shoes were a greater problem because she had never worn them while in his care. He had had to draw around Mia's foot with a pencil on greaseproof paper that he had in the kitchen, so that he might present the crude drawing to the shop to find something that fitted. At home she had always been barefoot, except for an old pair of his socks.

The shoe shop assistants were less sympathetic than Madame Oiswennier's. Eventually he bought a pair of the cheapest boots and hoped they fitted. The idea of wasting money on something that would not work filled him with disgust. He hated opening his wallet and spending his tightly folded money. Even though he knew that every penny would be reimbursed and that his employers never asked for receipts of the exact figures he was spending on their behalf. He returned with his purchases, trying not to notice that something was twitching unexpectedly beneath his disapprobation and anxiety. Something alien and totally out of place. Something like excitement.

Later he told Mia to put on her warmest clothes because they were going out, then sat back in one of the closest chairs to watch her reaction. She stood without a word and covered her mouth with both hands. Neither of them moved or spoke for a long time, and then he exploded in a spitting rage. 'Get dressed, your masters have ordered it so. Get dressed or I will lose my job.'

Nobody had ever shouted at Mia before and the effect was devastating. She slid her hands away from her mouth to cover her ears. She then realised that her mouth was bare and gaping, so she covered it again, which left her ears naked and vulnerable to more abuse. She rotated the flurry of her hands in a rapid, non-stop cascade about her flinching head.

Herr Aalbert watched in amazement. He had never seen anything like this, and felt he should be in hiding to see it, not sitting a few naked feet away from her without a wall to screen his unprepared arousal. Without thinking, he fled the child. In his bedroom he found an almost threadbare silk scarf that he had had for years. He rushed it back to Mia and stood before her and lifted the scarf up to cover the lower half of his face, bandit style. He saw that her eyes had registered this. He then lowered it to the height of her face. Their eyes met in a way that they had never before.

Her hands fell to her side and he very gently wrapped its lightness about her jaw and tied it behind her neck, just below the hairline. With the lower part of her face hidden and her eyes cast down, she looked almost normal.

'Miss Mia, get dressed, so that we might go outside for a walk in the park.'

She said nothing, but after a few moments turned and slowly walked to her room.

When she returned she was unrecognisable. He thought that he knew all of her clothes, from laundering them and from examining them when she was not in her room. But he had never seen any of these. She stood ready to go in a starched floral dress, woollen stockings and a floppy straw hat, the kind that an assistant gardener might wear. The scarf was still about her tiny face, which looked as though it were suspended beneath the hat.

He shook himself free of surprise and brought out the boots and the cape. She stared at them until he knelt before her and lifted her leg to ease a foot inside. He then tied the laces. Once both shoes were on and the cape negotiated over her head, her hands firmly clamped on the scarf and the hat at her feet, he stepped away. She retrieved the hat and screwed it back into place, then attempted to walk. It would have been humorous, if either one of them had possessed a sense of humour. They might have laughed together or shared a coy embarrassment. But her hobbling attempts to walk and his anxiety about the failure of his rudimentary plan only produced a grim frustration.

'You will have to hold my hand, when we walk together, do you understand?' he eventually said.

She tried not to understand but did, and offered up her thin white paw. It vanished in his hairy talon, which sucked up the little warmth in her hand and tried not to snap it. By the door he reached for his hat and winced as he glanced at the notepad on the wall. The single word scrawled like a threat or a promise stayed in his head even after they left the apartment and descended the curved elegance of the staircase, Mia in terror of the first physical height that she had ever negotiated. Her eyes darted and locked on every feature while he still blearily read the word pencilled in his head: Salpêtrière.

When he opened the street door the outer world buffeted Mia like a tidal wave. They stepped into the scent of wideness and the huge reality of day. The traffic in the Avenue Rogier shuddered and bellowed with a physical proximity that she had had no experience of. The sedate and muted transports that she had viewed from her high windows had nothing in common with these monsters of noise and stench. Aalbert felt her trembling terror in the palm of his hand, and his now uncertain future, and he gripped harder. She had forgotten him, even though she was pressing close to his body, wanting to hide beneath his coat.

It was then that he realised that they had lied to him, or at least given him a false impression. He had been told that she had lived in the apartment for a year before he arrived and he had assumed that her previous life had been normal; that she had simply moved there from another home. Now he saw that she had never been on the street before, never walked down a staircase. Never seen the wide world. Something in the dust of his heart plumed and he coughed, the cinder walls of his lungs shuttering under his vested skin. His hurried mind dug in against the emotion.

At least she would not run away. Quite the opposite; she stuck to him like a fly to gummed paper. He guided her further across the street away from the cars and towards a park full only of bicycles and prams. He guided her to a long cast-iron bench that looked as if its flowing lines had languidly grown out of a flowerpot rather than been spat out of a crucible. She jumped when she touched the cold unbending foliage of its supporting arm. He pushed her closer against it as he sat down, wedging her in. He straightened his coat while looking for words to cup her leaking fear.

'Look, see how big the trees are . . . Here.'

She did not respond because she did not know what a tree was. Everything was big here. Everything extended in all directions until it spilt itself beyond care and focus, under a vast, glowing cold sky.

'This is the Parc d'Avroy . . . It is very popular with young people.' He looked more closely at his silent ward and saw that the scarf was saturated and ready to fall.

'I will take you back now.'

She was out of the seat before he had finished the sentence. They walked back a different way, skirting the trees that enclosed the oval centre of the park. There was a change in her hand, a sudden flicker, not unlike electricity. It made him jolt and slow down but she moved on. Their roles shifted. She now led him forward towards the edge of the most astonishing thing she had ever witnessed. At its edge she stopped and started making a sound under the wet scarf. Her hand was firm and for the first time dry.

'You like the lake?' he said quietly, the surprise sweetening the edge of his voice that was now no more than a cobweb billowing in the breeze. She removed her hand from his in a single movement that he did not have the ability to stop. She knelt by the paved edge of the water and very slowly lowered her head into its surface. The straw hat disengaged and floated away, the scarf sliding sideways as her head vanished beneath the surface.

Herr Aalbert was frozen in disbelief. All his fears were happening at once, in slow motion a few feet before him. She was drowning herself and he was to blame. He stepped out of the nightmare and grabbed her thin arms which felt more solid than the cast-iron bench. He pulled up and back, but she did not move. Her spine was rigid. Her head had been below the water now for almost a minute. He quickly looked around to see who had witnessed this. Because running was still an option. Nobody except his masters and the concierge knew about him and the girl. This was the first time anyone had been able to see them together. A few silhouettes of distant walkers twigged the distanced paths. Nobody had seen them, he *could* run. It had worked before. If you run fast enough and in an unpredictable zigzag, then nobody will ever find you. He looked back to the girl and lost the time he had been away. How long had she been submersed now?

He yanked at her again and nothing moved except an old strain in the base of his back. Then he pushed her sideways and she fell over like a tin toy, partially lifting her head above the water. The tips of his fingers had turned blue with the surprising coldness of the water. He pushed again and she fell back away from the lake. She was stiff and hard and set frozen in the bend of her ducking posture. He pulled her forcibly away from the water's edge and knelt at her side, hastily picking dead leaves and scraps of paper from her face. Her mouth was wide open and her eyes were shut, and every muscle of her body was taught and inflexible. Was she dead? He had seen dead people this stiff before and he knew that crushed bodies often stayed in their weird foldings long after they had been retrieved from the accidents that re-shaped them. He tried to roll her onto her back, but she would not flow, only bend in an angular and unnatural fashion. Her legs bent upwards in the same posture as when she had been kneeling. He must escape this now, before it was too late. Then she spoke. Not a voice of the tongue or lips, hardly a voice of the mouth.

'Unku,' she or something inside her said.

Now he was trapped, he must take her back home. He took off his coat and wrapped it about her, rubbing it over her wet hair, which did little except produce a high slippery noise as the silk lining hissed and slid over it. He chaffed and slapped her face, and sat her in the closest position to upright that she could manage without tumbling sideways.

'Please come back, miss, please come back.'

He pulled his coat further over her and lifted her over his shoulder, her bony rigid joints digging in to him. He carried her like a sack of logs over his shoulder back through the park, across the avenue and along to the front door.

Once inside he set her down, still inside his long coat, and breathed deeply at the base of the stairs. It was not her weight, which was slight, that had fatigued him. It was the burden of responsibility that compressed and crushed him. He vowed that once he had her safe inside the apartment he would pack and vanish and leave all this strangeness for somebody else to fathom and clear up, and he hoisted her back across his shoulders, the ache in his lumber region growling in displeasure. As he ascended the stairs he thought he heard the click of the concierge door, beneath and at the back of the staircase. It was a despicable sound to him, like a camera snatching evidence of other people's lives.

In their hallway, safe behind the slammed front door, he struggled with the sodden laces of her boots. In her room he removed anything that was damp and placed her like a two-dimensional toy between the sheets of her bed. She was still frozen in the rigid angle. He massaged her jaw until it softened and closed, keeping his thumbs on her eyelids until they remained firmly shut. He wrapped a warm towel about her and put an extra blanket over her bed. A massive exhaustion was consuming him. He drank the last of the warming brandy and knew that he was too tired to escape that night. He would do it in the morning while she slept, if indeed she still lived. He crawled into his bed fully clothed and disappeared in a great wash of nothing. Even his dreams were too tired to mock and argue tonight, which is why he was surprised to find one curled up next to him in the first drizzling light of the morning: Mia, softened and wrapped about him. Outside, a disinterested snowflake fell past their misted window.

Over the next few days she never let him out of her sight. She pawed at his trousers and touched his hands as if she had never seen them before. He tried to withdraw, keep a polite distance, but she would have none of it. She sunk to her knees and held his ankles as he packed their suitcases.

She never left him, wanting physical contact or at least sight of him day and night. When he had to leave the apartment she would mew against the locked door, some thin part of the sound escaping under it into the stone staircase as he made his descent. She would be at the same place on his return, ready to cling and touch, the snow from his overcoat falling on her hair and thin shoulders.

The kind of affection she seemed to crave was beyond him. Impossible to reciprocate. He could not make the spark to kindle the warmth, no matter how hard their bodies rubbed or their disparate hungers collided. He became aware of how ungifted he was in gentleness and the wisdom of care. His clumsy wooden-ness delineated his shallow knowledge and made all attempts at feeling awkward and stilted. Embarrassment sullied their bed as much as her saliva.

And for her part their transactions were stupidly gloved in innocence. Just the slightest sight of acquiescence in him became a declaration in her eyes of tenderness or formal manly affec-tion. As the streets thickened in snow and the telephone remained silent, a gnawing sense of panic filled his waking hours. All his routes of escape were being sealed off. He was being isolated, and something like guilt was again stirring in his atrophied soul. Signs of unmitigated emotion were leaking in the corridors. The apartment was shifting out of his control. He would be blamed for everything. He would be found out. He would be punished. It had happened before. He had to escape, to leave her constant presence and the apartment that contained his enforced cohabitation. He would lock her away safe in her room, inflicting a mild sedative to help her become drowsy and uncaring about his departure. But since their disastrous expedi-tion outside, he dared not lose sight of her, and she him. Even his nights had been stolen. But most deeply missed were his moments at the secret listening spots, when he would catch her at her toilet. The thrilling distance and his power of invisibility was infinitely more pleasurable than her affectionate pawing and her tight, breathless embrace. Then the lens of the wall's brick, plaster and floral paper amplified his appetite by focusing the wrongness of his knowledge of her: a delicacy of separation.

Sharp and citric and so unlike the obvious bluntness of actual contact.

Now he yearned to walk away. To look at another human, one that needed nothing of him, to sit in the bar or dissolve himself in the Bruegelesque throng of the Sunday market. It had been weeks since he had watched the dancing in Au Metro and drunk himself silly from eight in the morning to mid-afternoon. He urgently needed the tobacco fug and lunatic adult clientele of the market's most infamous bar. He knew of course that in this dismal weather the dancing bar would be packed. This made its memory shine all the brighter.

But he dared not go as he waited on the eve for the telephone to ring, for the directions to be given for another departure. And she was so strange now, he should never leave her alone. This made the allure of the bar even greater. When something cannot be had it often increases the desire to obtain it, perversity working like a distorted lens in the path of the weakest rays of an oblique sun. And that's what began to burn in Aalbert's dry, tinder brain.

Two

YELLOW

When God gave the first humans consciousness, as they shivered their way out of Eden, he whispered advice under his celestial breath: 'obscure thyselves.' Every tribe of the sons of Adam and every half-simian with ingenuity has since learnt to brew or distil fluids, vapours and powders in order to relieve themselves of the intolerable jabber of thought occasionally; to numb their senses just enough to sensually smudge judgement and nerve. A good bar is a sanctum to this need. Au Metro was a cathedral.

Liège still had dignity on the rim of its poverty. This was the armaments centre of Europe for hundreds of years, but the cordite trade had long since been stolen by the East, leaving only the empty shell of industry behind.

Many in the Sunday market had left before dawn and trudged miles to be there. Some came out of the tangled Ardennes, escaping the drudgery of thankless labour in small, inbred fields of stubborn family crops. They brought baskets of this or a rucksack of that in the hope of a trading for a good morning's drinking. A chance to dance and talk and fuck out of the mud of their home patch. The dance and the market were the alibis of desire, objects and voices pawing at each other, swelling the passions of human meeting. To some extent the trade was incidental, only helping to curate a vast nomadic museum of history and food that cherished the odd at its centre. There is always a gritty pearl compressed by such life, a transmutation hutch where fiction grows in direct proportion to the dwindling of fact. Au Metro was such a gem. There it was impossible to imagine a fiction larger than the incident occurring at the next table. Alice and the Red Queen could *petit déjeuner* there. Their prime ugliness and alienation would be relished, their quest for the impossible expanded.

The dancing began at 8.30. By 10 the over-enthusiastic, the already horizontal, and the jabbering harmonica player were being gently shovelled outside. Au Metro was not big enough for a stage or a pit, but it did have a shelf, jutting out from its back wall. That's where the hunched musicians were folded, hard up under the peeling ceiling. Their lacquer heads and taller instruments scraped the over-painted cobwebs. From there the crabbed sway and pulse animated the circus of dancers thundering between the tables: the couples; the brave lonely; the *demi-mondaine* with their attendant beautiful teens, Arab-eyed in a wisdom of innocence that knows all, unsmiling and waiting for their next dance to be purchased. The toothless old men danced in their seats and even the Flik joined in; two of whom, drinking at the counter, suddenly agreed and removed their gun belts, handing them over to the barman (Wild West style), unable to resist the charm of the strident puppetry.

The minstrels' shelf was cleverly tilted backwards so that any musician who lost their purchase or sobriety up there did not tip forward and fall, or maybe nudge the resident band's vocalist over the edge. Because, following good musical hierarchy, he was at the front of the troupe with just enough space to kneel, while giving full reign to his voice and expansive personality. Drinks were passed up to the band on a thin metal tray that had been nailed to a short pole that looked like it may once have been a broom handle. This act was skilfully performed by one of the cafe's three waiters; a trio that were only alike in the similarity of their total extremity.

Bo Bo was a six-foot-four-inch transsexual, caught permanently somewhere in an intermediate stage, where both realities are furthest from belief or resolution. Bo Bo beamed down onto the exhausted tables of drinkers that she has politely served for years, her stubble splintering the pancake, her milk-blind eye smiling into the next glass of pastis. She constantly tried to hitch up the bass of her coal-bunker voice into a phlegmy falsetto, to match her coquettish gaze that declared constant, genuine shyness.

Her companion Monsieur Edmund was older, an ink-wash of a lounge toad starched with Dracularian elegance; the ancient white hair dubbed into negative, a blue-black ink trickle of it pinned under the arm of his heavy spectacles, their tint even darker.

The third was called Celeste. She was the fastest and the most dangerous to cross, and seemed energised by the cut and thrust of the customers' demands, a middle-aged strong-boned woman of smouldering sexual potential. She was obviously owned by nobody, or nobody that any of the customers had ever met or seen. There were many rumours, especially among the lone drinking men whose sly eyes never left the curve of her service; the balanced squeezing between tables and dancers that never went without a concealed surge of longing.

One of the most discreet of these was a tall fair haired man known as Lawrence. Everybody assumed he was from elsewhere because of the way he spoke and moved: a gentleman perhaps slumming, or a writer gathering characters for some unfinished fiction. The loudness of his deferential politeness nearly disguised the lupine hunger in his downturned eyes.

Celeste never allowed herself to catch the stabs of his eyes; she was far too busy earning her wages and deserving her tips. She possessed the unique talent of being able to take an order long before the customer had finished announcing it. Twirling away from the table while they were mid-speech, in a harsh wisp of her constant perfume: Lily of the Valley. In other circumstances this might be labelled rudeness, but in Au Metro it was understood as efficiency. When the order was eventually delivered it was always right. Even when it was not, this was understood and respected by all the regulars, who greatly relished the ignorance of any passing drinker who would dare to complain about an error.

The three waiters were the heralds of a cast list that could only ever read as fiction. Their ornate humanity guided, served and protected their patrons with wisdom, care and humour. They could deal, and had dealt, with all manner and species of drinker. Excesses of voice, violence or abnormality firstly spoken to with the concealed whispers of M. Edmund. Then a discreet extraction as Bo Bo lifted them out of their seat and escorted them to the rainy street, with the gentle firmness of a cat carrying her kittens in the shielded ferocity of her velvet mouth. If this was not enough then the waitress stepped in between all speech and argument and finished the unpleasantness with an abruptness that all turned their gaze away from.

The Earwig needed to be there, escape and be there again. He had spent most of his life avoiding humanity, especially crowds. But Sunday mornings at Au Metro were very different. The heaving proximity gave him invisibility. He could enjoy the intoxicated pressure of his species because they did not recognise him as one of theirs. He only made the pilgrimage once a month, but recently the severe new duties with the child had stolen his own pleasure outside.

He had become irrationally obsessed about it and with that obsession had grown an anger against the child who prevented it. So this Sunday morning while she slept he tiptoed into the kitchen under the baleful witness of the refrigerator, which groaned and muttered against his clandestine action, even before he took the pills out of his dressing gown pocket and crushed their whiteness in the grey metal mortar that he normally reserved for black peppercorns. He mixed the gritty powder with elderflower cordial and a spoonful of condensed milk; a combination of opposing fluids that Mia had recently taken a great liking to. As the concoction coalesced he made coffee and then carried both cups into the large silent dining room with the tall windows that overlooked the avenue. Dawn had risen in a yellow sulking sky that was equally laden with slate grey banks of featureless clouds. The cold clarity of night had been bullied away by it and by the neutral light that now flooded all. The city was beginning to limply move about inside it and the peeling bells had just started to call the faithful to Sunday prayer. He pushed cotton-wool balls in his ears to dampen their effect. He stood and peered down at the shallow activities, knowing that four blocks away, towards the river, another more frenzied life had already been seething for two hours. Down there, the frost that still etched the contours of the avenue and distant park below had been driven off by the clustering warmth of the masses, pushing through the overcoated, white-breath stalls. He ached to lose his contours among them. To wrap and dissolve his meaning in their swollen woollen sea.

A glassy sound from the bedroom announced that Mia was awake. He looked into her cup and finished his own, which had grown cold and bitter. She was returning from the bathroom as he approached the bed. She fell back into the sheets, extending one thin arm towards him. He ignored it and placed the cup on the bedside table close to her face. Only her fingers seemed to be aware of his proximity and they fluttered and curled as if to make contact. Her eyelids had already returned to agitated dreaming.

'Drink now, it is morning. Drink, then you can rest some more.'

The fingers stopped moving and the taut muscles in her arm redirected it away from him and over her prone body, with the hesitant velocity of a toy wooden snake – the kind that is articulated in equal sections, each being held to the other by a pinched leather hinge, thus giving weight and inflection to the semblance of unpredictable but purposeful animation. The fingers touched the glass and waited.

''Tis Sint Maarten day,' he said.

Her hand closed around the glass and conveyed it to her mouth without her eyes opening. Beneath the breath-thin lids, Mia still wallowed in the sight of another world. She drank the concoction in a single steady stream and let her hand and the glass subside under her chin, and after a while it rolled off her bony jaw and fell into the sheets. He stood helplessly above her for twenty minutes or so, or at least to when all the distant bells became still and frozen again. He then pulled the blanket up over her deeply sleeping body and left the room in longer-growing strides, the elasticity of escape pulling his limbs into action. He dressed and gathered money, tobacco, keys and two tiny white balls of oily cotton wool. He locked Mia into her room while checking his pocket watch against the upright clock in the hall. He estimated that he had up to four hours before the sedative started to wear off.

It was colder outside than he had anticipated and the wind ignored his layers of clothing and viciously sought the tepid marrow of his thin bones. He gathered his topcoat about himself and headed quickly down the boulevard and across, through the stiff trees of the Boulevard Piercot towards the curved cleft in the city where the great Maas flowed. He reached the Quai Paul van Hoegaerden and followed its path with the loud river sounding below him.

He smelt the market one block before it became audible, the stalls of hot pastries and chocolate entwining with the damp sawdust of the animal cages. The sizzling pork and the steaming clothing louder than the shuffle and gaggle of the crowd. It overpowered the damp green shellfish stench of the fast waters. Then it became visible in the faroff bend beyond the smouldering Bridge of Arches, and his crusty heart jumped like a child's. He was going to be enveloped in a grown-up menagerie of stink, failure and desire, and the anticipation of it overwhelmed him with joy. It was at that moment that his watch slurred, its arms resting on lazy elbows, its tick slowing to a tock.

BLACK

Saint Martin's day was a poultice to all manner of infections and barnacle-like obstinacies. It had started before dawn in the great church and spilt out into family homes and the street later in the day. But inside the bar its holiness was unsung. Better to raise a swilling glass to the saint's Halloween-like festival and all the exchanges of nakedness that occurred during its masked pageant.

Most of the tables were already taken. Only two seats were vacant. One was next to a swaying woman, whose movements were exaggerated and elastic; the other was next to somebody reading a newspaper and seemingly indifferent to all that was taking place around him. The choice was simple, and Aalbert pushed his way inside, squeezing past the buoyant flesh of the dancers that occupied all the standing space. He exaggerated his thinness and desperately tried to show that he was not affected by their thundering gyrations.

He finally got to the chair, which was placed beneath a coat stand, some of the hats there still relinquishing the last drips of dawn from their dense, shabby felt. The Reader ignored his arrival and the little signs he made to ask polite permission to share the table. So he gave up and sat down, placing his smoking equipment on the scarred circle of marble and ordering a drink with three simple movements of his fingers (a well-practised gesture for regular users of the bar). He sat back and lit a cigarette and discreetly adjusted the balls of gooey cotton wool in his ears. He then examined his fellow customers: a few known faces, but no horrors, nobody that he had to avoid. The Ricard and water arrived along with a dish of olives and some small salty biscuits, all cunning ploys to produce a thirst in the bar's customers. It was wasted on him; he intended to drink as much as possible in the three hours that he had allowed himself. He nodded his thanks to Edmund, who acknowledged him with a slight tucking in of his neck and the tiniest blur of his indifference; it said 'known/safe/respectful solid drinker but a poor tipper'. Aalbert's first three drinks didn't touch the sides. He changed tactics on the fourth and decided that his 'thirst' needed something a bit more profound. So he ordered Triple Vow, one of the infamous high-octane beers made in a nearby monastery, for which there is no agreed sane gesture of the hand.

He had swilled half of the potent beer when the music stopped for a while and the dancers found room at the tables, and the bar became overworked.

'The true reason that our dear brothers in the Trappist order say nothing is because they can't.' The voice was warm, familiar and tantalisingly allusive, in the way a forgotten name is when on the tongue but not remembered clearly enough for speech, even though its quality, meaning and taste can be perceived.

'Do you know that you are drinking their silence?'

The voice came from nowhere and demanded Aalbert's attention, which he reluctantly focused. Then the newspaper was slowly lowered in the manner of someone who did not want to scare anybody or anything near it away. Aalbert grimaced. He was sitting next to 'a Talker', the worst species of neighbour for a professional drinker to endure. Aalbert looked at the man smiling at him and knew that they had met before. But the stranger's clothing was far too expensive for anybody he knew. His immaculate haircut and grooming was fastidious and expensive. On his left hand he wore an ornate ring with a dark, blood-coloured gemstone.

'I am sorry, I did not mean to disturb your pleasures. Sometimes I just say the first thing that comes into my head.'

'Um . . .' said Aalbert, trying to remove his eye and demonstrate his lack of interest.

There was something about this stranger's voice that seemed to be passing straight through the tight balls in his ears as if they did not exist. The alcohol was working on him, the edges of things becoming amiably indifferent while their centres and purpose became elated, exuding pleasure like warmth.

'Do you frequent this establishment often?'

'No, not much,' said Aalbert.

'I think it's my first time?'

Aalbert tried to look more closely at his new companion. There was something admirable in a man who was unsure about his previous whereabouts. And there was something about his voice that was reassuring.

'I am mostly a stranger in these parts. I live in Paris. Do you know that city?'

Aalbert shook his head and put his nose back in his glass and mumbled that he did not.

'I have a charming residence in the sixth arrondissement, in the shadow of Saint-Sulpice.'

Aalbert ignored this detail and its afeared turn towards the facts of another person's life. The stranger somehow became aware of his new companion's distaste and switched the subject instantly.

'You know I have never tried one of those. I don't much care for silence.'

Aalbert agreed without a word.

'Are they stronger than the Ricard you were drinking before?'

'Yes, and better at quenching a man's thirst.'

He looked admiringly into the near empty glass.

'This is the Triple, you know?' he said, and drained the last drop. 'There are two strengths below this one and three above.'

'Really?' said the stranger, who had folded his newspaper with precision and put it somewhere out of sight.

'Are you an expert of such things?'

Without a doubt, Aalbert nodded. 'Yes, I have experienced many different makes and strengths.'

'Ha, a connoisseur!'

Aalbert made a depreciative curve of his hand.

'Perhaps, sir, you might recommend a vintage for me?'

Aalbert suddenly smelt a rat. Was this oily stranger soliciting for drinks? Was his interest no more than a ruse to gain a free beer?

'You see I have been drinking champagne and quite frankly it seems rather anaemic in comparison to what I normally drink.'

He was holding his glass in the carefree way of a man who might just toss it aside, when the dim light from outside glinted on its silver rim. Aalbert now saw that this was one of Gervas's famous set, the six royal flutes he kept in a glass-fronted display case behind the bar. Gervas had once been the sommelier of a noted restaurant in Cologne and the glasses were the last vestige of this previous eminence. Famous in the bar, they had never left their little museum before as far as Aalbert knew and he was truly impressed. Who was this stranger to command such respect?

'SO!' he yapped with such force that the Earwig nearly dropped his own heavy baroque goblet. 'So, what are we going to drink, my friend? What do you consider best of the mute brethren's genius?'

Aalbert noticed that while he spoke the stranger's gleaming black eyes were seeking out Bo Bo's milky one. Aalbert knew what he wanted to order. Westvleteren XII, the nectar of the famous abbey of Saint Sixtus, was a fabled beer that he could never afford and Gervas had claimed he had never sold any, with a strong sneering suggestion that even if any of the rabble in Au Metro could purchase it, he would not sell it to them: '*Perlen vor die Säue werfen.*'

'Even better in Dutch – "*parels voor de zwijnen*" – don't you think? I am surprised to hear you use Fatherlandisch when you are so clearly from the lowlands.'

Aalbert was unaware that he had said anything out loud, but the confusion of that was washed aside by the gratifying wave of flattery. Whoever this stranger was, he was a man of acute acumen.

'Yes I am . . . but, my parents . . . were . . .' He stopped under the shadow of Bo Bo's looming attention.

'Please order for us and I will be delighted to pay,' the stranger said kindly.

Aalbert looked up into the odd countenance and spoke the magic words. Bo Bo leant closer, trying to read Aalbert's lips, making sure they matched his speech.

'Perfect choice. Please may we start with two of those, if you please my dear, and why don't you have one for yourself,' said the stranger.

Bo Bo understood every word of this outlandish request. Dumfounded, the waitress curdled up a blush beneath her harsh chalky foundation, because the voice had flattened and scraped up a gob full of local gravel so it sounded just like her own.

'Excellent.' The stranger's voice slid back to its previous smoothness.

Aalbert watched the order being exchanged at the bar, fascinated to see it so readily accepted.

'I think it's time we introduced ourselves. I am Rey Tyre, a pilgrim in these parts.'

Aalbert's attention was still at the bar when the stranger made his announcement. Did he say 'retire'? Was his name the act of leaving? Giving up the profession of life?

He looked into the stranger's face, but found no answer. The dark gleaming intensity of his eyes made the rest of the stranger's features seem vague, out of focus, like trying to see beyond the close proximity of a candle flame. Maybe it was the previous Triple that had caused this effect.

'And you, sir?' asked Tyre.

'Aalbert Scellinc.' And his name sounded empty in the bar's confused air, like the carapace of some departed insect.

'May I call you *Albair*?' The voice pronounced his name in exactly the same intonation, but with a French inclination. And before he could answer, Tyre continued, 'I have the feeling that we may have met before, but I cannot think where. This is my first time in your fine city. Do you travel much? Maybe in the war?'

Nobody had ever asked him so much about himself in such a short time. He avoided such intrusions, generally by having no social contact. But when contact had been pressed upon him he always tried to remain aloof and guarded, hoping to give off a radiance of invisibility. If he were ensnared by another's personal questions then he would change the subject instantly. So what was happening now, how did things reach this stage? Before he had time to answer or dissemble, the silver tray of black bottles arrived.

RED

*A*nd the saturated pillow was full of dreams, spilling and slop-ping, so that each feather became soggy and drowned. Its deli-cate springy stem turned to mush. Mia rolled over, escaping the pillow's suction, and spilt some of her enforced sleep across her face.

But this did not wake her. The rooms and corridors outside ticked and wrenched with the extremes of temperature. The grand boiler in the basement of the building pushed warmed air up through the wrought-iron vents to keep the apartments at something like a comfortable temperature, while outside the world was cooling. The first few flakes of snow drifted languidly down to touch the inhabited plane, a silent drifting coldness that would soon enslave the continent. From the core of the rooms another cold heart pumped noisily as if crudely applauding the changing external conditions. The grumbling refrigerator coughed and shuddered, the few lank vegetables and sullen milk juddering against the trays of hundreds of ice teeth.

Tyre asked Bo Bo to join them. 'If she has a moment to spare?' After getting a wave from the bar, she agreed and sat sipping at a crème de menthe, her chosen tipple. They sat and chatted and ordered another two rounds of the excellent beer. Tyre seemed genuinely pleased by Aalbert's choice, and appeared to be enjoy-ing investing his money in the afternoon.

The room began to change around them and eventually the musicians crawled back into their places on the shelf above. This was a sign for the giant waitress to return to her duties, which she did with a dainty flutter of thank yous.

'A remarkable creature, a wren in the body of an ox. What do you think, would she take or give?'

The question confused Aalbert, and while he was trying not to think what the answer might be, Tyre began to fillet him again. 'It may have been in the trenches. I can see you better there covered in mud, wading in the shit and blood.'

Was the Earwig hearing this correctly? Or was the drink twisting them? Was Tyre mocking his accent and lack of education? The words had been smeared in a dialect that he recognised as that of his home town.

'I know this song,' shouted Tyre over the insistent rhythm of the polka. 'Da rum da rum da-da!'

Aalbert sipped at the brandy chaser that he did not remember arriving.

'Do you ever wonder what it must be like to be her?'

'Who?'

'Our friend here who hovers between bird and beast. Imagine waking and being her.'

Aalbert had no answer for such nonsense.

'It's what you all want,' Tyre said smirking. 'Every single human being, everywhere on the planet.'

Aalbert felt an unfamiliar line of disgust sneak inside him.

'What, to be like THAT?' he spat.

'NO!' Tyre's voice had changed again. 'No! Not to be like that, but to want to know what it is like to be somebody else, just for a moment, to step out of you and become somebody else. See the world from another mind. Every human from Eskimo to tycoon, from fishwife to Hottentot all have the same impossible desire. It is one of the few constants you all possess.'

You?

Aalbert had nothing to say, but his mouth shivered as if it did. Some of the dancers came swirlingly close to the table and the old man shot out his hand to protect the glasses.

'Da-rum da-rum. Da-rum da-rum!' Tyre shouted at them and they laughed back. 'Da-rum ta-dum. Oh, I think she is waking.'

Aalbert attempted to focus hard on Tyre.

'What, who?' he slurred, his voice faint below the swirling crashing dancers.

More people pushed in from the wintry streets outside, shedding their thick coats, steaming with cold. Some even began dancing before they drank.

Another tray of beers arrived at their table and Tyre pushed notes into Bo Bo's gigantic hands. The floor shook with the weight and unison of the heavy mob's mania. Tyre was laughing and clapping his hands.

'Humanity, oh, humanity.' Then he looked at Aalbert as if he had just seen him for the first time and said, 'Your wife, she stirs.'

This time Aalbert was onto it, grasping the meaning of the words before they danced off around the room.

'I have no wife, you are confusing me with another.'

'Are you not confusing yourself with another?'

'I don't understand you."

'You nearly had a wife after the war.'

The music was getting louder, its pounding rhythm giving no quarter, chairs and tables were shoved and jostled, glasses were skidding. Tyre's large ring was tapping his glass in rhythm to the dance. A large woman spun into Aalbert's back and bounced against its instant rigid hardness. She did not even have time to apologise, so fast were her contortions. He spat abuse under his breath while shouting over it.

'I have no wife.'

'Aalbert, you don't have to lie to me. I make no judgement.'

Tyre's eyes glittered even brighter as if their black centres actually projected jet.

His ring was tapping the glass louder, making it sound like a distant bell.

'There, she turns again,' he said waving a flutter of fingers into the thick air, as if stroking somebody. Was he talking about the fat dancer? Or was he . . .

'She was called Marie, the other one.'

'I HAVE NO WIFE!' he blurted out just as the band stopped playing and everybody subsided ready to drink and breathe normally again. His declaration caused a second of stillness just before the entire congregation fell into hysterical, tear-jerking laughter. He shrank under the humiliation and seethed with a dry, virulent rage. Tyre pulled a pantomime face of shock, placing one long finger over his lips to silence the Earwig while the ring finger rattled the glass into a pointed alarm. Behind the hushing finger Tyre whispered, 'It's your new bride that is turning, *the child* that is awakening, not the old one. *Not Marie whom you burnt alive.*' Then he took the finger off his lips and pointed it at the Earwig and shook his head in comic disapproval.

Aalbert was out of his chair and turning the heavy table, spilling drinks and glasses in all directions in his rush at the stranger. He grabbed him by the lapels, dragging him upright so that he could head butt him; a technique that he had delivered many times to those who so deserved it. He yanked Tyre hard, but instead of his face coming in range for the crippling blow, he just floated upwards. The man weighed nothing at all and Aalbert's force had lifted him far too high, so that the hammering butt missed him completely and passed through the arch of his own rigid arms, making him lose balance and fall badly. Tyre had settled and just stepped aside. The mob were unsure exactly what they had just seen, took the only joint, mutual response possible and bellowed with laughter.

Aalbert kicked out in skidding rage, trying to stand up on the slippery floor. His hand was bleeding from broken glass and he had crushed his cigarettes in the process of climbing upright again.

'Bertie, what are you doing?' said Tyre, who was standing behind the imposing presence of the waitress called Celeste.

Only his father and his long-forgotten Marie had ever called him 'Bertie'. How had this stranger known her name and his diminutive? A fear of exposure joined with his burning humiliation, and a congealed sluggish violence forced its way out of his being. He wanted to tear Tyre apart, to find out how he knew so much by picking the information piece by piece out of his dissected body. But instead he blurted out something completely different.

'Stop saying it, PLEASE, stop saying it.'

The words burnt his ears. Why was he pleading with this cunt when he only wanted to kill him?

He dug the stained cotton wool out of his treacherous ears to hear Tyre speak. When he did so it was in the timbre, pulse and intonation of the waitress who had come to protect him: 'But I said nothing.'

Tyre had the fingers of his left hand tucked under her belt and inside the waistband of Celeste's skirt, demonstrating intimate ownership in the way of a child or a lover. Bo Bo had come up behind Aalbert and softly put her huge hands on his arms with the intention of guiding him out of the bar. But Aalbert was too fast and unpredictable for her and he slivered away from her grasp. From behind the waitress Tyre simpered, 'Bertie? Bertie?' as if talking to a naughty child. Then his voice swallowed itself and with the awful clarity of a bell said: 'EARWIG.'

A great torque of spite ran through Aalbert. In less than the time it takes to read this sentence, he grabbed the neck of one of the bottles that had broken when he fell and with all his might charged with it into the face of the malignant stranger. Tyre saw it coming and twisted his fist into the waitress's belt, pulling her before him so that the razor sharp, thick black glass gouged through her lips and nose. The force of the impact was mimicked by the bright spurts of blood that sprang from her ripped face.

Tyre shouted, 'Να Τηζ,' an archaic form of Greek for 'Be Her'.

The room buckled and tipped and Aalbert came up on the other side of shock inside Celeste staring out at an animal version of himself attacking her. Blood filled his female mouth and his female brain and the pain tasted better than anything he had ever known. The world re-shaped itself as he was ripped apart, shock met sweetness. More wool fell out of ears. Everything was red as understanding and blood fell out of his eyes.

'υποστηρίζω' – 'Return' – Tyre shouted, and the room toppled into a normality that had never tasted so bad. Aalbert was back in himself staring at the wrecked face of the waitress, who Tyre was holding up. It was only then that he saw that Tyre was shoeless, his naked feet varnished by dripping blood.

Every particle of Aalbert Scellinc echoed apology for every second of his life, all that had gone, all that was occurring now and sickeningly all that would occur in the future.

Then Tyre, in the London tongue, screamed 'RUIN RUIN,' which Aalbert heard as 'RUN RUN.' And he did, pushing all the stunned dancers out of his way. Two drunken policemen attempted to retrieve their gun belts from behind the bar, but he had made the door and pushed into the thronging market crowd. Whistles were being blown from the door of the bar as he slowed and forced himself into the human tide that pushed between the banks of loud, overcrowded stalls. Towards the end of the market he left it and turned north, escaping into the empty side streets that led towards Rue Léopold.

The bad weather had divided the city, those that were not partying together or jostling in the market were at home. In the empty street all sound was stolen by the falling snow. Only his heartbeat and his rushing, muffled feet might have been heard in the empty freezing streets, where the snow had settled fast. Drops of blood fell from his hands as he fled. He only noticed this as he scurried into the Place Saint-Denis and stared in stupefaction at the vividness of the red, black and white at the end of his pale wrist. He was still clutching the night glass of the bottleneck, saturated in sticky blood. He dropped the weapon, and started to wipe his hand against his coat. Then he saw the fountain in the middle of the square, half frozen but still dribbling water from its elaborate candelabra of ice. He tried to wash his hand in it but it was too feeble, so he rubbed it against the ice, smoothing the blood away. He twisted his head to and fro, looking for witnesses of this unseemly act, and with each gesture he shed a swathe of memory.

He looked again, but nobody was there. The grey vespertine streets were frozen bare of populace. Anyway, what difference would it make if he was seen smearing the ice pink? He had just committed a violent crime in front of an entire bar full of witnesses, including two Flik.

But he hadn't seen a soul since he had run away and he knew his trail must be cold by now, everything else was. Better to be cautious, though. He looked around again and tried to rub life and dryness back into his freezing hand. His clothing refused to offer up any warmth as he walked on into another flurry of snow and the general direction of the cathedral bells that had just started calling out over the growing darkness.

Mia had been awake for nearly an hour. The telephone rang from the hall for a long time. It had never done this before and she did not understand its meaning. She knew *he* was not there because the sound could have only be meant for him and nobody else was moving in rooms. He was either there or not, so to find out she roamed about the bedroom continually trying the door handles to the passage and bathroom. One was locked and the other open. Then she returned to the bed and pulled the sheets back, hoping that this time he might be there, and that she might curl in his hands. She repeated the cyclic action again and again. Because eventually she would find him. He would occur where she had not looked for him.

She stopped at the sink in the bathroom where she gazed into the mirror, without registering that anything looked back; very much in the way that the long-term beast in the zoo unsees all those that attempt to engage their attention. She examined her mouth, the practised fingers worrying at the lack of teeth and her tongue, frantic and nude, missing the sharpness of ice and the volume of its temperature.

Ten minutes later all the sound changed around him. His feet clattered in the high-walled street. He tried to step more lightly, but the echo only increased.

Then somebody turned into the other end of the dark street. A hideous, stupid face bobbed and flickered towards him. He slowed and dug his guilty hands deep into his pockets. The approaching illuminated face was circular, its large mouth grinning below an engorged and ruddy nose, squeezed into grotesqueness by equally flushed cheeks. The eyes were insane and gleeful, not unlike the last expression of Tyre – an image that still floated detached and causeless inside his mind. Like the man in the moon, the face glowed in isolation and gave no impression of what the body beneath it was like. A few more paces on and he saw that it had the hands and gait of a child. The swollen face was a lantern, candle lit, carried by this boy. Aalbert crossed the street to avoid any kind of contact, and as he did so, two things happened: he remembered it was Saint Martin's day and forgot why one of his hands was so cold.

The boy carrying the traditional lantern at head height on a stick ignored everything about the Earwig other than the look of dismay he showed on seeing the flickering lamp. The child felt that this was enough to demonstrate that his part in the festival was already a great success.

Aalbert tried to behave normally. He even tried then to smile back at the child, to demonstrate how sympathetic he was to the moment. But the expression that drew itself across his gaunt and anxious face would have curdled milk, and the child looked away and gathered speed.

In the next street three more lanterns appeared, each slightly different in their physiognomy and size, but all loudly staring. Aalbert could not stop looking at them and each confrontation shaved a layer off his memory so that by the time he reached the next street with a stream of children, he had no recollection of any of the violent events that had occurred in Au Metro. By the time the procession had thinned out, he had forgotten that he had been to the bar at all. Only the face of Tyre remained.

He was four streets from home with a growing sense of stress about his unusual lateness and his usual sense of guilt flaring out of proportion, when the rider appeared. A hugely bearded man wearing a mitre and carrying a crozier sat upon a tall bay horse, whose steaming breath snorted before it, dragon-like. The apparition headed straight for him and he cringed as the bishop raised his staff as if to deliver a justified crushing blow.

'Peace be upon you, my son, the blessing of holy Saint Martin is yours.'

The Earwig shivered under the benediction, as the horseman turned and rode swiftly towards the procession, the place where his army of lantern-bearing children awaited.

Full night closed in around the horseman's departure and heavy snowflakes could be felt and heard more than seen in the shadows. Yes! He could hear the snow falling, the crispness of auditory power had returned. He walked on, feeling a great weight had been removed. Was it the blessing of the carnival saint?

He was almost home, the key already in the palm of his now warm hand, when he remembered his lessons of the saints and Saint Martin in particular. How apt it now seemed, the Roman soldier discovering a poor naked man at the city gate in deepest mid-winter, his compassion tearing his cloak in half, so that he might give protection with this act of shearing.

Aalbert put the key in the lock and yanked at it, entered and closed the door on the hostile world behind him. As he mounted the broad stairs he tried to remember other details of Saint Martin's life, but could not. Only a picture hovered out of focus in a far corner of his mind. A hut on a tiny island, no more than a hump in the sea. The hermitage of the saint when he sought refuge from heretical sects that wanted to end his life. The picture must have been in his schoolroom. He stood before his apartment door, hours late, and tried to focus on the ornate little banner or label in the corner of the image. And suddenly there it was, gold words inscribed on a scarlet flag: *The isle of Gallinaria in the middle of the Tyrrhenian Sea.* He felt pleased with himself and he entered the apartment. Mia heard him arrive and rushed to the door. Aalbert suddenly stopped, another detail of the picture made him ignore Mia's approach. A tiny spike of memory or something like it trapped all of his attention. Something known and vaguely uncomfortable about the island. No, not the island, the sea. Its name: Tyrrhenian. Something familiar. But he knew no thing or person with a name anything like that. And yet a tincture of unease was there, without him understanding what it was, recognised yet tantalisingly allusive, in the way a forgotten name or word sits on the tongue but cannot be remembered clearly enough for speech, even though its quality and taste can be perceived.

He took this enigma with him to bed. Which Mia insisted on sharing. There it metamorphosed into a memory of a woman, the sound of a woman fading back along an endless river of floating stones. And a distant fire that cleanses everything. Mia slept curled at the end of his bed, one of her hands holding his bony ankle. One of his feet was holding her down. Pinning her at a suitable distance. But she whispered in his dream, in a voice she could never have. Speaking in the coil of his inner ear, the place that does not understand sounds and words, the place where fluid and tiny hairs balance stability. In there she or some being said:

'The holy book taunts and talks in confusions. Many think the King of Tyre is not a monarch of an obscure island, but the King of the abyss. Satan himself.'

Three

WHITE

*I*t had been snowing for a week now, ever since he had returned home from somewhere or other. He had left the apartment only once, to fill bags with food just in case the bad weather set in. The week turned into winter and there were rumours about it worsening. The newspapers told of frozen rail tracks and lost trains. The journey he had been told to plan seemed more and more improbable. He watched the telephone, waiting for it to demand. Weeks passed and still it did not ring. Since his late return that day, she had not let him out of her sight. Day and night she stayed far too close. He had started to dread the night. Under the sheet and blankets she would curl herself against him, her hands probing his body like a rock climber on a new mountain. He was diminishing under her touch.

From the beginning his manhood had refused to respond, no matter what he consciously felt. It seemed to have its own moral restraint. There was none of the interested twitching that the glasses pressed to the wall had always instigated. Proximity hobbled him and was now threatening castration. The dramatic change in temperature had not helped. He was shrivelling away to nothing, so that on some nights when his mongrel bladder barked awake and he had to pad along the shivering corridor to the unheated water closet, he could barely find himself, and stood fumbling and pinching in his pyjamas while the thin pipes giggled with ice and the refrigerator in the kitchen shook so deeply that it made all the crockery shudder in nudging, unlit chuckles.

Yes, the snow outside was getting worse. The entire firmament was being milled into snow, the stiff clouds splintering, the thin light snapping. The day and the night grated into falling ice, the very stars shredded to snow.

The Great White that overcame the unsuspecting planet only lasted a little under two months, but in that time it managed to wipe out a twentieth (although some said less, and others more) of the population. Central Europe suffered the most. It started with mist and ended in blizzard, but it was the dense fog in between that undid the poor lungs of so many citizens. Influenza was also carried in its blindness, and it sought out the weakened survivors of the last world war. It also mercilessly preyed on the new-born optimism of young parents who dared to believe in a new age.

During the Great White the bare streets echoed like a skeletal xylophone. Families huddled around meagre fires and lost their shapes and meanings under layer upon layer of clothing and blankets. Fuel was scarce and for long periods only a few dim candles and strangled gaslights showed that anybody existed in the shadow dwellings of the city.

In the last few hours of the working telephone lines, the phone had rung and left sparse details of the arrangements that had been made to keep them alive and sealed in the apartment.

The voice also tightly questioned him about the Sunday that he had forgotten. But it seemed to know more than he did, so the spindly interrogation was pointless, the long bleak spaces between the questions and the answers explaining more about his total lack of memory than anything he could ever say. It must have been the drink? The voice knew that he had been to 'a certain bar' and for how long. It seemed he had been caught red handed, and had not the faintest idea if it was true.

A boy walked through the white streets. His name was Pedric. He had carved a living out of these icy conditions. Pillage was spilling into the white laden streets as the outer roads and the train lines became blocked and it had been arranged that he would bring them food, logs and kerosene, all of which were wrapped in sacking to disguise their value.

Pedric was earning a small fortune as everybody else slid towards liquidation and starvation. His skills as a forager and purveyor blossomed under the patronage of Aalbert's invisible masters. The money they paid kept his young strength up and made him resistant against the impassable snow. He bartered and clinched astonishing deals with the diminishing shops and stallholders, whose few withered goods had become precious and rare. He burrowed and dug rat-like passages among the banks of frozen snow and manipulated others to help him make at least a slender part of the Avenue Rogier passable. His efforts were mostly ignored by the occupants he so diligently served. He was never allowed inside the apartment on the third floor, and was spoken to like a dog or a serf from behind the locked door.

'Just leave it outside,' the old voice said.

'But, sir, it is not safe out here. It could all be thieved.'

'Then you'd better leave quickly,' the gruff voice said without a trace of care.

'But sir!'

'BE GONE.'

Only after the street door was slammed did Aalbert unbolt and inch open a chained sliver of access to the apartment, his keen ears and watery eyes testing the space on the landing outside. Only when he was sure that nobody was there did he release all the latches and step out to retrieve the precious goods.

But Pedric was a curious fellow and wanted to catch a glimpse of his patron's most important tenant. So on the last visit, after he had pretended to leave, slamming the front door loudly, he then slipped off his galoshes and tiptoed back up the draughty stairs. He lay close in the depth of the steps, out of sight, peeping up through the bannisters and waiting for the door to open.

When the Earwig opened the door to snatch at the goods, Pedric was not surprised by the shifty leanness and darting sinew of the old man. It matched the foulness of his temperament to perfection.

There were no surprises about him, but there was a world of shock about the shadow behind. For between the old man's leaping grabs another figure hovered in the hallway, staring out of the apartment with beautiful anxious eyes. The little flinches that her hands and arms made towards the old man each time he stepped outside were seen by Pedric as involuntary stabs at escape. Later, on the icy steps outside, Pedric began to formulate an impression that the girl he'd glimpsed was held against her will by the old and cruel man; a maiden imprisoned by an ogre, that he, Pedric, might be able to save. And as he considered this, his fleeting memory of her face changed, incubating into an effigy fleshed with grace and perfection. It glowed so warmly in his brain that it melted the falling snow around him in a mobile aura. Love began to unfurl in an uninhabited cavity of Pedric's life, a sweetness to give to him purpose. He looked back up into the falling snow, towards the tall street door and then up further to where the rooms that housed the treasure must be. Curtains were being slowly pulled against the night and his desire to see more. Something about the slowness of their closure worked in reverse, as if they were lofty distant flags unfolding in a solid and bountiful wind, giving grandeur to his epic purpose of seeing her again, his hope of releasing her from this abominable imprisonment and making her his own.

He pulled himself away, because this night was over and the sooner he worked and slept into the next time he saw her, the better. He was planning his campaign as he pushed through the white tunnels and skidding ground, planning how to hide and how to meet her away from the horrible old man, planning a tantalising seduction that carried him right into the disappointed cavity of his dreamless sleep.

PINK

*T*here was no claustrophobia in the white blurred days that engulfed the apartment. Mia's demands and proximity increased continually, filling their enclosure with a viscous tenacity. There was something like security there that Aalbert did not really understand. No one was looking for him and no demands were being made outside of the tall rooms.

But intrusion from the outside world came with the delivery boy, and his increasing attempts to instigate a conversation. Aalbert even began to wonder if there was more to it than had first appeared. Perhaps he was some kind of spy or junior police-man. Such things had been whispered about in Germany. Or maybe a civic guard. Malicious lies might have been told against him, sniffling accusations of fictional misdeeds.

He decided he could handle such things, he had before, and this wretched youth with his darting and inquisitive eyes would get nothing out of him. There was no reason that he or the child had to exit their retreat until they were finally sent for, and God knew when that would be. He had things under control. There was no need to worry.

And then she started drooling and sobbing. The ice teeth were sliding out of her mouth on a sticky tide of fear and dismay. At first he thought that there was something wrong with the refrig-erator, or was there perhaps a fatigue in the constantly used moulds? When it came to the teeth's application he helped her push them harder into reinforced gums.

But it was not working. They no longer fitted. Something was changing.

He watched her trying to realign them, her wet fingers becoming frantic with failure. And while she writhed with the miniature struggle, a button fell from her blouse. At first he thought it just another tooth, but he saw its pearly gleam slither to the floor at a different pace. He got up to look at her closer and saw that the button had not just fallen off but had been yanked. He reluctantly looked closer and saw the tell-tale tension across her taut chest.

Over the years the child's insistency had forced him to avert his enquiring gaze. Her intimacy had provoked a distance in him that kept him uninvolved and emotionally aloof. Her recent hugging closeness made him keep his eyes on some imaginary distant mountain or the wafting movement of a cobweb high up against the peeling ceiling.

Now he looked and saw to his horror that the teeth were falling out of her gums, not because they were shrinking, but because her gums, her mouth and every other part of her body was increasing and forcing itself into the more inevitable mould of womanhood. Aalbert's gaze deflated and toppled from her body onto the carpet and gleaming button. An exposed pearl distancing itself from the grit and mollusc of its creation.

Mia's agitation with her mouth increased and she started to talk through her fingers, pleading with him to help. He pulled himself together and remembered the manual and the tools that were in a walnut box. He had used them before for minor adjustments in the way he had been shown. He retrieved the box from the chest of drawers where it had remained forgotten about for the last two years. He took the carefully folded paper and smoothed it flat on the dining table. The mechanical pattern of her gums and the metal and gutta-percha fittings were clearly delineated.

Mia changed when she saw the box and stood up to come and greet it. In all the adjustments he had made before, she had never once flinched from the obvious pain, never struggled against the intrusion of the instrument. Rather the opposite; she had given herself up to them, pushing forward to encourage the contact. Fear was never part of the process, and she appeared to suck on the brittle agony like a normal child does on sugar.

The gums had a tiny jewellery-like contrivance grafted inside them, so that each socket could be adjusted by the turning of a minute metal nut. This would in turn adjust the 'clamp' of gutta-percha to squeeze the gingiva into a tighter resistance. Each socket also had a surgically constructed inverted flange, so that the bulbous ridge on the root of each of the ice teeth would engage, after it had been forcibly plugged in.

Aalbert shooed her interfering hands away and started to lay the tool out on a red rubber tablecloth that had also been inside the box. He dragged the reclining chair across the floor to the table and set its creaking spine backwards. Mia had already collected towels that were needed to soak up the blood. He had done this once before and knew how long it would take, so he collected his bottle from the kitchen and pointed Mia back into the bathroom to make her ablutions before settling down. He ignored the refrigerator's comments and put the brandy and glass next to the instruments. He carefully assembled the hypo-dermic, and drew the morphine solution into its measured tube. He had never used it before, but the instructions suggested that it might be necessary. He wiped the needle and laid it gently aside as she came out of the bathroom smiling.

She had never smiled before, ever, and the strangeness of the expression on her impish face was unpleasantly disturbing. She also had a new, coquettish stance. Mia looked back into the bath-room and then straight back at Aalbert, as if scooping something from there to flutter it before his eyes.

'What's wrong? What have you done?'

She grinned even more, tilted her head on one side and made for the chair. The weight of her constant need seemed to have been sloughed off. Without taking his eyes off her he made for the bathroom door and pushed it open quickly, as if to catch something red-handed. Nothing was there. She was already wrapping the towels around her neck when he went inside, now slowly checking everything for damage or change. Everything was completely normal, until he lifted the noisy lid of the toilet seat and heard her giggle outside. The water in the bowl was pink.

Pedric had been to the apartment three more times since first glimpsing Mia. He had never been invited inside and he knew he never would be, so he took his time delivering the goods and then skulked about the landings without any real purpose other than the need to exercise proximity and curiosity: a fearful combination reminiscent of Poe's Imp of the Perverse.

> 'There is no passion in nature so demoniacally impatient, as that of him who, shuddering upon the edge of a precipice, thus meditates a Plunge.'

He found himself pressing his ear against the thick door or unconsciously sniffing for molecules of her presence. Most of all he anticipated, imagined her coming to the door, alone and in need of his company. But he had always left disappointed – until today.

He had brought another flagon of kerosene and was beginning to wonder why they used so much. Just as he was stooping down to place the metal canister close to the door, he heard the first noise. It stopped him dead in his tracks. It was her, and she was making a sound evidently produced by an extremity of feeling.

He had only seen a woman climax once; seen and heard it from across a shared room. Heard the animal voice of the deep-rooted quest that should only belong to pain. But then it had been coated with honey, and sheathed in excitement. (Why was he thinking this here?)

Then he heard her again and it gagged the focus into hurt. The old man was hurting her! Pedric pushed his ear against the door and caught further sounds. The old man was mumbling angrily then she yelled a hollow scream, and it pushed Pedric back from the door in a bewildered shock. After a few moments he grabbed at the bell pull and yanked it back and forth into violent reproach. He could hear its frantic clatter inside and heard the old man swear.

Previously the bell had only briefly teetered on its spiral spring, apologetically responding to the timid request from the outside world. Now it shrieked and bayed its demands. Aalbert removed his hand from her mouth with such shocked force that it nearly lifted her out of the chair.

Pedric braced himself for the attack. Aalbert threw open the door and screamed into his face, 'HOW DARE YOU! HOW DARE YOU DISTURB ME SO?'

It was not what the youth had expected and he stared open-mouthed at the old man in the rubber apron. One of his claw-like hands was gripping the edge of the door in a tight rage, the other hung at his side holding a thin, curved steel instrument. Both hands were bright with blood. Then Pedric's eyes flickered to the blur behind the old man the end of the corridor inside the flat. She must have followed the shouting to the apartment door where Aalbert stood screaming out into another world.

'YOU IDIOT, HOW DARE YOU!'

Pedric spat back, 'What are you doing to her?'

The old man was just about to bring the tool lunging up at the throat of the insolent youth when she touched his arm, and with this tiny gesture Aalbert turned and looked down at her.

'Go back inside,' he said.

Pedric's instinct to attack the old man was also drained and replaced by incomprehension at the child's affection for this monster. Also by the total shock of seeing Mia in the flesh; a flesh that had stepped clear of his luminous illustration of her. Her eyes were enormous, the meniscus of them almost broaching their thin lids. Her face was pointed, motionless and without a trace of colour. Only her mouth was moving in a weird chewing independence, which dribbled to show that it was full of blood. She stared up at Pedric with an expression like pantomime outrage and he almost laughed at it.

There was no doubt that the threat from the vicious old man with the metal dagger was nothing compared to what this creature could unleash. There are moments in human lives where all understanding becomes vacant, and that sudden departure of knowledge allows wisdom to step in its over worn shoes. The relationship between gnosis and will can be swifter in its action than any other. So it was here that Pedric, with a speed on the other side of alarm, extended his hands: one to the old man's hand and the other to the hand of the child on Aalbert's arm.

His voice said, 'Pardon.'

The dryness of the Earwig's hand and the moistness of the girl worked like the opposite poles of a galvanic battery sending the youth flying backwards and falling over the flagon of kerosene. Aalbert had slammed the door shut before he could raise himself and look back. The commotion and the thunder of the door must have been heard echoing through the entire staircase, because sounds of other doors higher up could be heard. The muttering of other tenants came drifting down. Pedric gathered himself, ashamed and damaged, and slid back into a street that was reassuringly empty.

The old man was shaking with rage, fatigue and desperation. Mia had primly sat herself back in the chair and tucked the stained towel bib-like around her neck. Her mouth was open and she was anxious for the torture to begin again. Aalbert poured himself a stiff brandy and sat down heavily, waving a 'yes yes I will be with you soon' hand at the girl. She nodded, grinned and sat further back in the reclined chair. The tightening operation was not going to plan. Two of the four metal nuts that he had adjusted had sheared off. All the areas he had attempted to rectify were copiously bleeding and he could not see if the fruits of his labours were succeeding. He was out of his depth. She needed the same professional who had set the gums before. He finished the brandy, picked up the tool and went back to her mouth. It was drier now and free from running blood. The damage inside made his testicles shrink and he was about to give up when she steadied his hands with her own and guided them back to the wounds. He worked for another thirty minutes and then fled to the lockable bedroom, where he kept his crate of spirits.

He drank until the sounds of her wet fists pounding the door became distant, abstractly rhythmic and without meaning.

The shadows in the apartment, the boulevard and probably the rest of the world were all becoming whiter, colours were draining under the filter of slate clouds. The blues lingered the longest, displaying their affinity for polar conditions. It was the last rind of beauty on a torrent of indifference that had no memory of colour and possessed an automatic longing to carry that amnesia into the stead of humans. The warmer greys were next; the hopeful gullies where an echo of yellow once hid.

Pedric made sure his next delivery was fast. He placed the goods outside the door, rang the bell and was gone before the door could open. That's the way he would work from now on. He would try and remove the girl from his mind. He would not see her or that monster again.

That's what he planned, but on the next delivery they were waiting for him.

The botched surgical adjustments were going from bad to worse. When not in the chair with the old man's hands in her mouth, Mia was becoming constantly distraught with the lack of adhering teeth. And all the teeth in the fridge were pink now, her frozen saliva being continually tainted by blood. Aalbert was beside himself. He needed help. He needed to make contact with his masters so they could send a surgeon, jaw mechanic or some kind of other proper tooth man. The telephone hung against the wall like a great black apostrophe. He had asked himself how he could contact them. Then it had become clear. That idiot errand boy must be receiving communication and money from them. He must not scare him off again. He must catch him at the next delivery.

So Aalbert hung about the inside of the door during the times that Pedric normally came. Occasionally he would open the door to peer or listen out, then when he heard the sound of someone approaching, he slid out of the door and pressed himself against the wall of the landing that was blind to anyone approaching the apartment door, pushing his bony shadow back into the space where he would trap this idiot boy delivering the kerosene.

Pedric placed the canister down with the fluid slopping and sucking inside. He then pulled the bell knob and turned quickly to escape. But Aalbert stepped forward and blocked his retreat, saying, 'One moment if you please.'

Pedric looked horrified, his eyes flickering past the old man for a way out.

'We need to speak.'

The youth was ready to dart in any direction and would knock the old man aside if necessary.

'Please, *we* need your help.' Aalbert had his hands raised, much in the manner of a man trying to catch a bird.

The emphasis on the 'we' made Pedric turn back to look at the door, and there she was. He was caught between them. In a calm but firm voice the old man explained that the girl had a problem with her mouth and needed the attention of a trained medical engineer or dentist. The young man looked back and forth between the speaker and the girl. Sometimes Aalbert pointed at his own mouth and then at her. She opened her mouth each time.

Pedric was scared of his gaze being hooked on the girl again. He had to tear his fascination away from her, so that he could keep a wary eye on the violent old man.

'We need you to tell our masters to send somebody immediately.'

'Masters?' quizzed Pedric.

'Those that tell me and you what to do.'

The young man pulled a prolonged face that convinced Aalbert that his impression of grocery boy's intelligence was more than accurate. After a long while this expression closed, as if a long wire inside him had been slowly pulled taut – much in the way of a change in the face of a ventriloquist's dummy.

'Ah! You mean the pigeons?'

Now it was Aalbert's turn to ape the face.

'They don't like the snow.' Silence. 'It freezes their wings.'

The next time the boy called the old man wearily let him in. He had no desire to argue, carry provisions or hide the girl, who now hung about the front door when she was not weeping and rubbing her mouth. After he had dragged the goods inside, Pedric just stood there staring at Mia who glared back. He had lost his incentive to rescue her, and was now ensnared in the sticky strangeness of the situation, without any real understanding. The powerful moanful girl and the bitter caring old man confused and excited him. He had become addicted to all their contradictions.

'I sent the bird back with your message.'

Aalbert did not reply, just hissed bristled abuse. He had not bothered to shave over the last few days and his general demeanour had lost something of its sharp angularity. Only his ridiculously long shoes seemed to maintain any momentum, even though he was wearing them without socks and the laces untied. He grimly pointed for the boy to leave when the telephone rang in the kitchen. All three stared into its direction and then in unison stared at each other. Aalbert broke free and rushed down the corridor. He lunged for the phone and unhooked it just as it stopped. He slid sideways, stumbling to the floor beneath the dangling wire of the swinging pendulum. The youth was standing, nervously grinning in the doorway, which Aalbert instantly misunderstood.

'Little shit,' yapped Aalbert. The boy looked blank. 'You LITTLE SHIT, shit, shit.'

Pedric did not understand what the crazy old man was saying. His vitriolic English sounded like bad French; another erratic outburst of mania, in which it seemed he was now demanding a cat; 'cat, cat, cat.'

Aalbert was trying to scramble to his feet, his shoes squeaking loudly on the linoleum floor. The telephone had almost stopped moving when he heard the click deep down in its wire. Somebody on the other end had only just hung up. To his horror he realised that the dangling instrument had been listening to everything and like a sickroom thermometer had absorbed and recorded the exact colour of the event. He had shown his true self to his masters, who now must be outraged and distrustful of his usual loyal, discreet servitude. He sat in a deflated heap, staring at the black hanging receiver, which had transformed from a tense, aloof cypher into the sated head of a vengeful cobra, exhausted into a torpor by satiation.

GINGER

$\mathcal{M}$ia heard the soft rapping first and thought it was the fluttering of a moth, so light and persistent in its nature. She left the bathroom, where she had been standing on a rickety stool to see herself in the mirror of the cabinet, and slowly walked towards the origin of the sound, one hand clamped over her mouth. The lofty apartment was still, holding itself in its classic refinement against flaking decay and its present occupants. She padded down the long corridor and then understood it was the front door that was making the noise.

She stopped and waited for the bell to ring, but only the flutter continued. It was not the boy, the boy who made her change shape inside.

Every time she saw him now it happened, and the feelings of it lasted longer and longer after he had gone. For a moment after his last visit the feelings even stopped the ache in her face.

The shape inside must be squeezing her, forcing the blood out of each end of her like a flannel when you squeeze the middle.

She knew Herr Aalbert did not like the boy. He always screamed at him and made faces, so she knew something must be wrong with the shape and the feelings that he had made in her, even though it tasted of sugar and welled up like pain. Or the thing like pain that made her face crack open and unplugged her silence with those noises. *Lufting*, Herr Aalbert called it.

The *Lufting* that came about the boy was not the same kind. It was shorter and heavier than hers, which made it last more in the walls and the floors that sucked it in. Sometimes she held it, closed in her cupped hands, so that she could keep it longer and enjoy its funny smell. Even now, remembering, it made the shape inside her and she almost forgot the noise of the door. The next sound washed it all away; it was a tiny cry that sounded like her. Another like her was there trying to get in. Then it sounded again: tiny, far off, lonely. She pawed at the door and the fluttering stopped. She wanted to open the wood and meet herself.

Herr Aalbert was sleeping and she knew never to wake him. Each time she'd done this he had become very cross, which made him clumsy with preparing her teeth. She needed to find a way to get him to open the door, but she didn't want to go and wake him up. Then she had an idea. She ran back to the bathroom and dragged a stool from there and lumbered it until it was roughly under the shadow of the bell. She then clambered up onto it and stretched with all her might, her pink stubby fingers straining to make contact with the cobwebbed bell on the graceful curve of its spring. But she was too short.

Her next determination was even more astonishing. If the stool had been her conceptual Himalayas, then retrieving the umbrella from the hall stand was her Everest. She tried to hold the heavy thing while she climbed, but very quickly discovered that she needed both hands to yank herself into the first perching. She dropped it several times in the process and had to climb back down each time. Eventually she managed with the use of her knees and gums to gain a standing with the umbrella on the rickety stool. She waved the thick black stick above her head until it bludgeoned the bell out of its repose and into a discordant, irritated squawk. She quickly climbed down, dropped the umbrella and hid further down the corridor.

Aalbert stumbled out of his dream and into the reality of everybody else. He trampled over the umbrella and nearly walked into the stool. Mia watched every movement with gleeful surprise as he hurried to let the other one of her in.

Standing outside was a small man in a bowler hat. One of his hands was still hovering as if to continue his ineffectual tapping, the other tightly gripped the carrying handle of a small wicker cage that he held far away from his body, desperately avoiding any contact with its small noisy occupant. The Earwig and beetle stood examining each other either side of the door frame, much in the way that a reflection examines its other in a hall of distorted mirrors.

'F'nelt Rostlink. Doctor F'nelt Rostlink,' the beetle said in an understated tone which barely hid his belief that the proclamation of his name should send all others to their knees and demand a fanfare of trumpets. Aalbert looked blank.

'I have come to view and rectify a patient.'

Aalbert's blankness turned to look at the cage, which had just started to hiss.

He was trying to assess how its occupant might be used in the doctor's procedures.

Dr Rostlink understood something of this question and did not care for it. With great purpose he put the cage down between them.

'I don't normally do this kind of thing. Delivering livestock is not part of the duties of a surgical odontologist.'

Mia had made her way out of concealment to discover her other self by the door. She crept up behind Aalbert just as the cage was put down. The hiss turned into a plaintive cry the moment they made eye contact.

'I was asked to deliver this to you when I came for my consultation.'

'What is it?' asked Aalbert in disbelief.

'I would have thought that was blatantly obvious,' said Rostlink, who was rubbing his hands together as if to wash away any trace of this distasteful chore. Mia moved closer into his sight as he said, 'It's a cat.'

'A CAT,' said the Earwig. 'Why do you bring us a cat?'

Before the doctor could answer, Mia had rushed forward, scooped up the cage and run back through the corridors into her bedroom.

'I was told you asked for it. "A cat," they said. I was to bring you a cat when I came to work on the child's mouth.'

'This is nonsense, why do we want a cat?'

'I have no idea and no interest. I am here to correct a human mouth, not to discuss cats. Now, shall I begin or leave? My time is precious,' said the Good Doctor, his hand fiercely retrieving the Gladstone bag, all traces of the previous humility in his voice cooked off by the heat of the doorway exchange.

Aalbert did not want to make another mistake.

'Come in.' And then, without conviction or pleasure, 'Come in please, Doctor.'

Mia did not hear the door close, so engaged was she with the cat, staring now into its wide eyes, she recognised a difference. Not the obvious one, that it was another kind of being entirely, but that she and it were different to all those tall ones that occasionally entered her world, and different especially to Aalbert who had occupied and shared all of her selfness up until now.

The catch found her fingers and the cage opened and she put her hands inside to touch something entirely new, like an unfound cleft or ripple in her own body. The cat moved into her hands, and a shape bigger than that brought on by the boy filled her from her toes to her optic nerves. She brought it out and held it to her once bony chest. It squirmed in against her warmth and a tiny part of her leaked out. The cat purred, and the change in its sound astonished her. There was only one thing to do, so she did, and purred back. This was the beginning of a profound and irrational friendship. She quickly took the little beast to her room and curled up on her bed with it tucked close to her chest. It did something extraordinary, and again Mia felt arousal. It gently pummelled her belly with its stiff, hard little paws and pushed its scrawny head into the scrawny parts of her body. This odd person showed love in a physical and direct way, as if it wanted to burrow inside her and become one. The delight she felt was overwhelming.

SILVER

*T*he beetle was unpacking his instruments on the kitchen table, having refused the Earwig's more elegant temporary operating theatre in the living room. The kitchen's austerity and simple harsh lighting were superior in his no-nonsense eyes. The proximity to flowing water sealed the decision. The reclining chair was carried with great huffing reluctance to a position between the table and the fridge.

'Now, fetch the child,' the doctor demanded.

But the child had no intention of being fetched. She and the cat had become inseparable. When the Earwig followed the doctor's command with contempt in his craw and angrily loomed around the door of the child's bedroom, demanding that she should go to the kitchen, nothing happened. Aalbert repeated his demand while stepping a little closer. The cat arched its small bristling back and as he extended his ready-to-grab hand. The little creature opened its jaws and spat long and hard at the tall man. He stopped in his tracks and laughed at its courageous nerve. He could have crushed it or torn it apart with his hands, or thrown it across the room, so insignificant was its size. Now Mia tried to hold it as it curled and became rampant on her breast. Aalbert overcame his amusement and was moving in to rectify the pest's arrogance, when he saw something that stopped him in his tracks again. The black and pink interior of the cat's mouth was completely without teeth.

He pushed his head closer to be sure. The hissing velvet trap was bare – only the tongue darted in the glistening cavity. Aalbert was pleased by this funny detail and he suddenly warmed to the humour of the erasable little man in the kitchen.

'Come, child," he said. "It is time to mend your mouth.'

She did not move.

'We can lock your kitten in this room while your mouth is being repaired. You want that, don't you?'

She held the cat tighter and glared at him, and he saw a resolve in her he had not witnessed since the incident at the lake.

'Bring it with you then, but hurry. The doctor is impatient.'

Mia looked at him and saw that he meant it. She stroked the cat and carefully put it back in its cage. She latched the gate and carried it with her towards the kitchen. Aalbert followed, smirking.

Rostlink had lit his pipe, found the Earwig's stashed bottle of brandy and poured himself a deep glassful. The child walked straight to the chair and placed the cat next to her on the table on the other side of the instruments. Rostlink frowned and was about to order the removal when Aalbert stepped between the seated doctor and the tabled cat.

'You did this too, uh?"

'Please move that thing away from my instruments. I don't want it in my way.'

'P'raps it wants some more.'

'More what? What are you talking about?'

'You did the cat's teeth.'

'What . . .?'

'You did its teeth too, the whole mouthful. Just like the child's.'

'How dare you!'

'A good clean job you did. No?'

'I DON'T DO CATS.'

Aalbert walked off, still smiling. The cat hissed as he passed and Mia opened her mouth.

Humour is eccentric and unpredictable. True, certain basic formulas will produce mirth in the majority of the population, and are much relied upon by professional entertainers. But outside those engines of cause and effect, other more oblique mechanisms to trigger the satisfaction of a smile exist. Conditions and incidents that have no direct relationship with the comic. Consider Aalbert now, back in the living room, standing at the window musing on the snow-clogged streets and darkening sky, mostly impassive, not bothering to hear the sounds from the kitchen, and then the odd flicker across his long dry face; smirks and puckers, fed by small hums and quick sniffs. Something in the dryness of his brain was sparking pleasures. And we all know that it was the pompous doctor and the de-fanged cat that somehow had ignited it. But it wasn't the visual image of the little man, pliers in hand, that tickled him so. Nor was it the sublime cruelty. It was something else, something that had never been connected or associated with smiling before; a chain reaction that bleached every link of its meaning with each new outburst. If that dry old repetition was dug out of his grinning head and examined, we would find nothing funny there. And neither would he.

GREY

A horrible nothing awoke Aalbert from his afternoon doze. Thick, sullen smoke hung throughout the rooms and in front of the window, its aromatic richness making slow landscapes against the glaring stillness of the sky. An itch was blistering beneath Aalbert's unconscious. Some little spite was gnawing his ankles. He rubbed them without paying any attention and then fished out his pocket watch. The surgery had lasted over three hours. He pulled himself together and stretched from his curved feet to his scrawny neck. Six tiny welts became uncovered as his socks were dragged downwards.

The doctor was sitting at the far side of the kitchen, still smoking his pipe. Mia looked dead and unrecognisable. She was very white, her eyes wide and staring, her mouth distorted and open in a puffed-up face that was without a trace of movement. Bloody rags were draped or hung about her shoulders and chest.

'That should hold for a year or two,' said the Good Doctor. But he too looked pale and slumped.

'Is she . . .'

'Sleeping, yes. You had better carry her through to her bed. She will be like this for hours.'

Aalbert moved closer and touched the ghastly sight, expecting to recoil from her chill, but she was warm. She did not respond to his probe. He glared back at the doctor.

'How is this sleeping? Her eyes . . . her eyes are wide open.'

'I have given her an injection to soothe the pain and relieve the shock.'

Now the Earwig knew he was lying. 'She enjoys the pain and is never shocked.'

The doctor looked found-out: 'I gave her the shot to make the operation easier,' he quickly said, reading the expression on the Earwig's face.

'EASIER?'

'Yes, easier.'

'How easier?'

'Easier for me.'

The doctor then heaved himself out of the chair and started to pull more things out of his bag. He laid them out on another table in the manner of a maid delivering a cold lunch.

'These are the new trays for the new teeth,' he huffed.

Aalbert knew nothing of the new teeth and demonstrated his perplexity with a minor limp opening of palms.

'You'd better come and look. There is a difference in them.'

Aalbert closed in on the table and peered warily at the gutta percha trays.

'Observe these little stems, they are there to create a small central hole in each tooth. I have adapted her gums so that now each has a stem that will engage with the hole. This is necessary for strength, now that she is growing.'

Aalbert looked worried and the doctor enjoyed it.

'Each socket of the gums is now plugged to let the stems nestle and attach. The plugs will dissolve over the next four to five days or so. I won't need to come back if she is cared for properly. At least not until it is time for her to travel, then I will change some of her ice teeth for glass.'

The doctor was out of his chair and overcoated as he mumbled more instructions. He returned all the instruments and other paraphernalia to his bulky bag, patted his pockets and made for the door. He stiffly went to make his departure'

'Keep her mouth free of infections with the salt water,' he said.

The Earwig didn't hear this.

'Cared for properly' had deeply offended him and now a prickly quiet blossomed between the two men. The cat stopped licking itself and looked around, and even the discarded button tightened its contours under the chair on the hard polished floor. Only Mia remained oblivious.

After Aalbert had carried her to the bedroom and tucked her snugly in, he returned to clean the kitchen and strangle the cat. He filled the new tooth trays with water and put them to cool in the bottom of the fridge, which he had turned down; no ice would be needed for a week or so. The machine clattered and rumbled at the outrage, but then slumped into a reluctant hum. Its subjugation greatly pleased Aalbert, who was still aching from the doctor's insults and itching from insect bites to his ankles, wrists and neck.

Nevertheless the day was looking up. The child's enforced 'sleep' would give him some freedom. No more visitors were expected and he now had the added joy of dispatching the cat.

He first toyed with the idea of drowning it. He had done this to a batch of kittens in his youth. Some coward had left a bag of them, blind and mewing in the passage of the premises he was janitor to. He was ordered to remove them. He could have just tossed the bag into the rubbish, but even his leather heart had some pliancy in those days. He wanted to finish them off quickly. And he had never done it before, so a buoyant curiosity sweetened the act. There were six kittens in the bag, all desperate, starving and chill. Little bony bundles of wet fur and blindness, only a few hours old. He decided that drowning in warm water was the best and most kind process, so he filled a bucket with water, made tepid with the aid of the big black kettle that he had brought from the cellar kitchen. He tested the water with his elbow, without knowing why. It was just an automatic something that he knew. When it was ready he dropped the kittens in and watched. Instead of welcoming the warmth, which must have been very like the womb that they had recently exited, they struggled against it, forcing their tiny mewing heads above the now agitated surface to bite at the air. They climbed over each other, seeking any purchase to keep afloat. This was not what he expected; he had naively imagined a kind of softening of their plight, a floating back to the darkness and warmth of painless non-existence. But that gentle departure had turned into a sickening frenzy, which he had to finish. He plunged his long hands into the water and compressed the writhing knobbly mass of wet fur deep into the water. But they even struggled against *his* strength. He squeezed them and held them down further as they squirmed and kicked to escape, tragic morsels of pure life, defending their right of existence. Tears filled his eyes, but not out of pity, a welling up from elsewhere.

Eventually, after far too long, movement ceased and the tangle in his sad grip gave in. He dug a shallow hole in the small garden and slopped the contents of the bucket into it, without the need to look or examine the thoroughness of his work.

That incident had sunk deep into his understanding and stayed there in a more profound way than all the horrors of the trenches that he would be forced to endure.

But all that was best forgotten in the face of his present task of strangling or snapping the neck of that savage little beast that was already glaring at him from its cage. He opened its gate and put his hand in, grabbing the cat which began to hiss as he pulled it out. Strangely it did not struggle but softened in his grasp, turning limp and wet. He quickly snatched at its head and wrenched it sideways, as if undoing a stubborn screw-capped jar. Nothing happened. The neck should have snapped like a bread stick as he wrenched the head, but it did not break. Instead it felt like a solid bottleneck in his grip, provoking a memory of dread. Something happened in his inner ears and converted the dread into a sound; a sound that caused repulsion to seethe through him. He clumsily changed hands, the pliant beast curving across his now violent need without any kind of struggle. He tried to pull the cat's tiny head clean off, worrying it back and forth, but it was as resistant as steel. Steel and glass was grinding between his ears and a wave of nausea made him drop the cat and grab his own stomach with one hand and his throat with the other. He jack-knifed and crashed to his knees. The cat watched for a moment, shook itself, sniffed the air and wandered off to find the child. It never bothered to turn around to see if he followed.

The Earwig lay for a long time without thought, looking across the plane of the floor. The wooden boards of the kitchen, the carpeted tundra of the far-off rooms. A landscape of infinity, where nothing moved.

The cat found the child and climbed up onto her warm bosom. It ignored the ghastly staring eyes glaring blankly at the dim ceiling. It extended and nudged its small body into her contoured shelves, eventually settling in the taut space between her neck, shoulder and jaw. From there it had contact with her torso and head simultaneously, and could share the pulse of her breathing and the flavour of her breath.

Aalbert attempted to sit up, but it was beyond him so he gave in entirely to defeat. The clock chimed the horizontal night away. He slept in the dreams of waking and lay awake in his deepest slumber. The wrong kind of peace settled in the apartment, with all its occupants severed from reality. With a soothing chorus purring between the cat and the fridge, and outside the snow falling again to seal it in.

Four

GOLD

'*L*ook, look how the sunshine swolds the hills.'

A great brightness filled the blue purity of sky. It pushed hard against the meniscus of it. Every colour rose up to be saturated and warmed in it. The trees shook the vividness between their leaves, cascading shadows. The very air laughed in the branches and tasted the myriad temperatures trembling there. Further off, the mountain arose from the hills, impossibly clear. Gleaming white caps suspended over bristling vineyards and sumptuous fields.

'Now it is running faster than the train,' the child cried as it pawed the warm windows of the carriage.

'Look Mumma, see, see . . .'

'Yes, Beatrice, now come and sit down.'

The mother looked at the other passenger. She was trying to draw their irritation into herself. If she was more annoyed than they, then everything would all right. But little Beatrice annoyed no one else. The day was too fine and all she had said had made it finer. The countryside was growing as it fled past the train's windows, and yes the child had been right, the good broad light had 'swold' the hills and everything else in that magnificent day.

From her seat in the corner of the compartment, draped in a light shawl with a long green silk scarf wrapped about her face, Celeste watched the child from the warp of tiredness and the weft of her waking.

Lawrence had given her this scarf on the eve of this journey. He was not here now and a faint panic stiffened the colours of the silk, but only for a moment. After sitting close to her for over two hours he had gone to stretch his long legs. He would be back soon. In that she could trust. She closed her eyes and let the warmth pass through the lids. She would conjure no panic here. That part of her life was finishing. Lawrence had taken almost all of her terrors away and now he was removing her from the origin of the woe that had so blighted her life. He had persuaded her with his calm voice and large comforting hands to pack up and leave Liège and to travel to his house in the country, for a long and sustained rest. Even after she explained that she did not feel love for him and that she did not think it possible for her ever to love again, he still continued to press his suit, with its promise of protection. She had never experienced anything like this and it made her instinct interrogate her quivering optimism.

Surely he had proven care and affection in the last few months. Even if she did not understand his overwhelming need to look after her and help her find some joy and solace in damaged life, she must recognise his dedication and respond to that at least.

A quiet had filled the compartment and allowed the rhythmic sound of the wheels and the iron track to rise up through the wooden floor and rock the warm air back and forth. Celeste opened her eyes and saw that almost everybody else was asleep or dozing. The child at the window had stopped eliciting attention and now just watched the speeding landscape in a semi-hypnotic torpor. The sun had worn them out. She envied all the sleepers, their all-embracing balm. Like so many other wonders of life, this balm was invisible, inevitable until it was removed.

Seven cars down the long train Lawrence was standing in the vestibule between seated areas. His thoughts were still on finally persuading Celeste to leave her tawdry life in that exhausted city

and escape with him into remote contentment. It had been difficult. For some reason beyond the ones that she could speak of,
she wanted to continue back there, living a shadow of a life. He
thought it might be the ghost of her dead child that tied her
there; the memory of unreached years stalking her.

He had first seen Celeste in the hospital the week after he had
buried his mother. It had been his last duty for his mother in the
loathsome city, in which he had been forced to live for the last
months. The doctors had insisted that she be brought here, to be
probed and worried in the lofty echoing wards of Le Valdor's
gothic fantasy. True, the hospital had an excellent reputation for
clinical care and the development of new techniques to help the
ageing sick, but it lacked the gentle isolation that he so much
wanted for the old woman, back in their home across the border
in Linay.

They had lived together happily with safety and contentment
in the beautiful house that she had bought on the far fringe of the
village after the death of her second husband. The moment she
had told him of that wretched man's death he had spat in delight
and immediately returned to join her. It was a very long way
from the poverty that they had shared and survived in the south
of France, of which they never spoke.

Nobody knew them when they moved into the obscure
wooded hamlet, and their modest wealth and quality of life kept
them aloof and clear of gossip or prying neighbours. He had
given up his worthless job to be with her every day, and she kept
him and the house in perfect balance. They finally had the time
and means to live with and for each other, which they did until
the day the black crab of cancer found a crevice in their
security.

It had been with a heavy heart that he closed up the house and
found his seat in the huge ambulance for the long, uncomfortable and expensive ride to Le Valdor. He estimated that nearly half

of their savings had been devoured by the hospital. He visited her every day and watched all the expensive treatment come to nothing as she shrunk with the tightening pain. He knew nobody except the doctors and found solace in some of Liège's bars, where for a few hours he might escape the dread and the stink of the hospital. He had only discovered Au Metro in the last weeks before his escape, in that time when all the paperwork had been completed, the death certificate giving birth to his rights of property to the beloved house in Linay.

The day he received the final papers he had trembled with joy as he carefully clad the document in a rich paper folder that he had purchased for the occasion. He also bought an expensive leather case; a music satchel with an elegant rod of brass to hold it closed. He would not need locks and keys; he wanted to handle this precious thing. The brown leather was polished and subtle and he hugged its elegant slenderness beneath his armpit. He had never owned anything like this before. And now he had it all, the house and the future contained in this slender case. Even the loss of his mother could not darken or dissolve his rising joy.

On that day in Liège, following the meeting with the lawyer, he had been walking on a narrow path by the frozen river. He clutched the leather satchel and moved away from the edge, into the subtle mouth of Au Metro whose lights seemed welcome and becoming. It was quiet inside as he shuffled to a table and ordered a brandy, allowing the warmth of it and the place to enhance his glee. Only the slight ache of loneliness haunted him. His mother had kept a good and gracious house and her companionship had gradually sealed over all the old cracks and cuts. He needed someone to care for him again in that way. He needed a wife. It was during these sombre reflections that the door had opened and Celeste had waltzed in in a blast of snow and wind. At first he ignored her as she slipped into her apron and only lifted his eyes when she confronted him directly.

'Your pleasure, Sir?'

He gawped at the woman from the cemetery, no longer stooped and forlorn over that tiny gravestone, but alive and vibrant.

'May I take your order, sir . . . another drink?'

'Yes, yes,' he replied and cast down his eyes, not wanting her to remember where they had seen each other before.

Over the next few days, he hung about the cemetery for longer and longer periods of time. On the third day she was there again and he hid behind a spinney of trees and watched. When she left he slithered up to the grave and read the name and dates of the dead child he presumed was her son. She returned again on Sunday and he marvelled at the beauty of her poise and grace for one so lowly.

Lawrence had been watching Celeste. In that time he had only spoken to her three times, generally about nothing, but once about her, asking her name and was she from this town where she worked every day? To his surprise she didn't recoil, but stopped, put down her tray and sat next to him, sharing a moment of trust and kindliness with a stranger. She asked his name and they shared a minute of coffee and tobacco, and he fell in love. He was unable to take his eyes off her ever again, especially when she was not there.

Since then Lawrence had only been to the cemetery with her once. There she had told him everything about her lost child, and he about his dear mother.

It had been ten years since the child, Oskar, had died of the tuberculosis. Ten years of weekly visits to the grave.

He had estimated that the first time he had seen her kneeling by the small, pathetic tombstone must have been another Sunday somewhere in the early five hundredth day of visitation. She murmured, her beautiful lips touching the unmoving earth. How could she still find solace or meaning in this act? Did she imagine the perfect child sleeping in a thin wooden box two metres below her shivering touch, or did she calculate the degree of black rot, each week peeling back to mouldering bone?

The next time, while observing from the trees again he felt his pity become tarnished by a brooding irritation that he did not want to understand; the quiet pause before a storm of anger. Why was she still so attached to this undeveloped life? The father of the child was some kind of nobleman (aren't they all?) who had befriended her while she was in lowly service and had fled back to his native homeland of Sweden before he even knew of the child's existence. The hardship of an abandoned mother – how could she bear to perpetuate this gruel of grief and memory?

After all, he had almost forgotten his own mother's corpse in the earth below. He had even forgotten to visit her nearby grave as he watched this new woman from the shadow of the leafless trees. All that was forgotten since *she* had been given to him and her disfigurement had made her his. No other man would want her now. Her hot blood on his hands had been the signature of his possession.

The land began to change outside the speeding window of the observation car in the last carriage of the train. Gold bars of light danced around Lawrence as he finished his cigarette and adjusted his cufflinks and the ridged knot of his tie, and started to make his way back along the swaying carriages towards Celeste seven carriages away in the rickety snake of twelve. The train was curving through a long glacial valley, following the contours of the rugged mountain on a narrow rim that was growing steeper, the solid land on the outside of the rails falling away into a precipice. At the point where passengers might become anxious – and those who still stood by the open windows did indeed shrink back from the magnitude below – the train shrugged and followed its inner shoulder away from the gravity-saturated light and barged into the core of the mountain. The tunnel was only a short one; an early practice piece, a limbering up of the engineering bravery that would later rifle through the massive granite hearts of Lötschberg and the Gotthard. But the modest Louette-Saint-Denis tunnel was still a great surprise to the passengers of the Liège-Paris express that day. The great gulp of darkness and the echoing smoke thundered through all the carriages and compartments. Then those who had been standing in the vestibules and observation car were almost tumbled by the shockwave of vanishing light. Pleasantly on the cusp of dream, Celeste covered her face tighter against the noise and darkness. The children in the same compartment fell back from the windows, their fear too raw to cry. The echoing sound of the tunnel only knocked the 'O' out of their open mouths, their eyes darting from the now blind windows to where their parents should be. Others slid about or yelped. The very few, who had experienced tunnels before, just smiled.

Lawrence was midway down the corridor of the tenth car when the light was being sucked out. He stumbled and put out his arms to grab at the narrow wooden walls. After a few moments he found his equilibrium and moved slowly forward, his hands touching the glass windows and metal fittings.

Suddenly he touched something that should not have been there. His hand snaked back. In the shuddering dark that was now choired with the smell of cinders and sulphur, he had touched ice. Black ice in this hot imitation of hell.

He was in the first class part of the train, with its warning sign Not To Disturb. All its passengers were pre-booked – some for special needs and requirements. The privilege to be able to pay for total separation seemed to Lawrence then a tremendous luxury, as his hand hovered near the door and its freezing cold brass handle. He had been born in the teeming back streets of Marseille where proximity, family numbers and poverty devoured any trace of solitude and reflection. The cold of the door handle became a satisfaction to him now. He touched it again and this time savoured its uniqueness, allowing it to run into his arteries. Then, in the shuddering darkness, he realised he was not alone.

After the crippling snow all the water that had so devastated the streets and parks was nearly gone. The vast tonnage of winter had quickly dissolved and was being sucked back into the Maas by the sun. Liège was becoming normal again. But crossing the Parc d'Avroy was still difficult if one ventured off the swept avenues. Small warning signs had been posted in the middle of the widest expanses of slushy grass. Many a good pair of shoes had already been spoilt.

The Batte Market had also suffered because of the flooding, the river almost drowning it in the first few weeks of the thaw. Its banks had breached and the swollen waters had lapped at the very door of the Au Metro.

Imprisoned in his bar, Gervas started to drink away the remaining stock. Would the Sunday morning hordes even remember Au Metro after so long?

Pedric had to start again. The Great White had been his making, his little empire of ice tunnels and illicit trading had gone. His King Rat power had been dethroned by the seasons. Most of the money he had earned was gone too, paid to his greedy and demanding mother. But he had saved a little; hidden a few hundred francs here and there. When he fingered the concealed money, he always thought of the girl and that wretched old man who imprisoned her. Were they still there? He had had no orders about them since the snow went. No more well-paid requests for food and fuel. He snatched up his cap and decided to make an unpaid trip back to that house and the door of many bolts, to see what had changed, and if the girl had escaped.

It was 3 p.m. on a fine windy day when he reached the apartment building and saw the concierge mopping water off the front step. Pedric waited until the man had stepped aside and then followed him on silent feet. They had done a little 'business' together during that winter, and Monsieur Benoit owed him a thing or two. Now the short, stocky man turned and was startled by the proximity of the smiling youth. '*Putain!*' he gasped, covering his mouth with one hand and flapping the other over his chest. 'You scared me to death!'

'Not yet, old Master,' grinned Pedric.

Benoit got back his breath and snatched up his broom from where it had fallen.

'There is no point in you being here, they won't let you in.'

The youth was about to ask why.

'Shut up for days now, not opening the door for anybody. Won't even speak to me when I shout.'

Pedric was about to ask when.

'Four days ago now, I took a paper up to him and never even got a "thank you" for it. Not that he ever did treat me with respect. Miserable old bastard. Not even a word.'

'And the girl?'

'Girl?' struggled Benoit. 'Yes, and the girl . . . the imbecile child. Yes, not a sight or sound of either of them. Gone to ground they have.'

'Might they have gone away?'

'Them? Never! Never go anywhere, never set a foot outside. He might get caught.'

'Perhaps you'd better look in the apartment?'

'Certainly not! Nothing to do with me, what he does to her, what goes on up there. And without instructions it all stays locked until I am told something different.'

And with that dismissal, the concierge was gone, muttering into the shadowed corridor of his small room at the back of the house. Pedric climbed the hesitant stairs, each step exchanging its meaning from the one before – shock, doubts, irritation – and by the time he reached the landing an irrational fear had him.

He stood before the apartment door, empty handed and now empty hearted. He had no reason to be here, no alibi of parcelled food. Water was dripping down from somewhere above, making a niggling patter that sounded like the skinny heartbeat of the old man on the other side of the door, but strangely far off and remote. Perhaps it was the late afternoon light that was dissolving the sharp angles of the architecture and settling the hard stairway into softer dimensions. Nothing to do with heartbeats. They were silent as the grave in there.

Perhaps they were gone. Could he trust anything old Benoit had said? He turned and began to descend the stairs, looking back all the while, when he saw something that made him stop and after a moment retrace his steps and stand close to the door. He put his ear to it and listened. He ignored the bell and softly knocked on the beige painted wood. No sound came from within. He knocked again slightly louder. Nothing. Pedric knelt down and put his hands against the bottom edge of the door and tried to tease out the sliver of paper that was lodged there, but could not gain a purchase on its slippery obliqueness. From his pocket he took out a slender folding knife and slid its blade between the wood and dug the note towards him. It was damp on one side and dry on the other. He opened it out between crispness and pulp. It was a receipt for a portable basket, and the date showed that it had been lying there for four days. He dropped the paper and stared at the door, while taking a small case of tools from inside his coat.

During the Great White he had found it prudent to learn new skills, often trading goods for favours and tutelage. He reasoned that it seemed only fair to use his most useful accomplishment on the customer he had fleeced the most. Whoever the true masters of this apartment were, they had little interest in haggling over price. He was always given the price he asked for, making the food and fuel delivered here the most profitable. His gratitude to the clandestine client had been amplified when he had met that savage old man and realised that if he had been selling to him direct, his profits would have been shaved to the bone. Because Aalbert Scellinc was the epitome of skinflint misery and he wore it in every fold of his voice and gesture in such a way that leaked beyond the door and into the world.

Pedric now began to enjoy the anticipation of what would happen next, what he would find, and started applying his long curved picks to the lock of the door that had always been slammed in his face. He remembered the sound of the long heavy bolts and knew that they were not in place; the whole secret world inside and maybe the girl too was held beyond by the brass gums and steel teeth of one lock. He twisted the probes and hooks until he felt a moveable resistance. Then he rotated the pick and the jaws came apart in a satisfying, metallic tut.

The freezing door handle in the hurtling train still held Lawrence's focus.

Its cold came from the neatly stacked waterproof containers on the other side of the door, each sealed to hold their individual quantities of ice. They blocked the entire entrance and prevented any casual ingress or access.

The workers of the train were always alerted to the needs of their 'special' passengers. They had 'not seen', or rather unobserved, all manner of peculiar behaviour and indiscreet incidents over the years. The quiet seclusion needed for this particular 'medical condition', which they had been alerted to, was nothing compared to the august depravities of certain of Europe's most noble families. It always inspired admiration.

They were to be 'left alone'. The instruction was simple, and Guard Visener was determined that it should be obeyed.

He was on one of his tours of duty when he found the shifty, loitering shadow embracing the door latch of the cabin as the train entered the darkness of the tunnel. Visener stiffened into every folded crease of his beloved uniform.

'Do you have a compartment in this section, sir?' Already knowing the answer and looking forward to the intruder's lie.

'I was smoking in the vestibule,' said Lawrence curtly.

Both men instantly knew they were adversaries and locked antlers in the narrow wooden contours of the pitch black juddering corridor. The extending tips of horn were already scratching wild calligraphy in the varnished walls, and knocking and smearing velvet against the glass before the next word was spoken. Visener had seen the look of contentment on this man's face when his hand was trying the door and the speed at which he withdrew the offending hand was also an absolute confirmation of guilt.

'This is not the vestibule.'

'I . . . I was making my way back to my seat. Why do you wish to know? Is there some kind of problem?' Lawrence's voice had become firmer.

'The problem, sir, is that you appeared to have intentions concerning that compartment.'

'Intentions? What intentions?'

Lawrence said this while lowering his head, moving towards a charge. There was no space for doubt or retreat; Visener saw this and twisted his neck to parry any sudden thrust.

'You were trying the door,' he said.

'I was steadying myself against the lurching of the train.'

'You were looking in.'

'This is outrageous. How dare you say such a thing?'

His acting was so good that he started to believe in it himself. And the natural ardour of a wronged man arose in him to counter the cunning of its natural predator, standing side by side in outraged innocence. For a second Visener halted. A dim yellow interior light came on in one of the compartments, and the curtains of one of the windows was dragged aside. A face twisted itself against the glass to see what was happening outside. Both of the antlered men watched its steamy smeared distortions.

Then the bright light at the other end of the tunnel found the lip of its entrance and sped into its hollow, casting a shadow of undark before it. Celeste felt anxiety lift and opened her eyes into the carriage as dawn arrived. The children also found their parents and hugged them tightly. The speeding tubular dawn illuminated the silhouettes of the men who had been shouting in the dark.

Lawrence seized it like oxygen. 'I have had enough of this nonsense,' he said. "I shall now return to my compartment."

He moved to push past the guard. The men became jammed together, the guard turning halfway between giving leeway and confrontation and Lawrence attempting to nudge his way out without displaying open aggression. They both stumbled backwards, towards the gangway connection of the previous carriage. Each man could now see the other's contorted face.

'I need to see some identity,' Visener shouted, one hand reaching for his standard issue truncheon.

Lawrence had seen the metal joining door over the guard's shoulder and was calculating how he might push his stupid head hard against its splitting rim. Then the full bore of the light hit them, a solid birthing of day that rocked their violent tableau into high comic relief. They both instantly saw each other and recognised their archetypes; an Officer and a Soldier, both behaving preposterously. All the previous acts, including the trespass of touching the door, became meaningless trivia and arrays of antlers shrivelled back into lank tufts of embarrassed hair, as their reflections rattled in noisy bright glass.

The protagonists' eyes spun away from each other onto the pulsating floor as they slid past each other without another word.

Pedric swiftly opened the door to the apartment just wide enough to slide in around its closure. He pressed his stiff back against the door and held his breath, listening for sounds of occupation. But everything inside was still and silent and set in a calm, soft light. The heat was stifling. The radiators had evidently been pumping into the sealed apartment, while the weather outside had shifted into an early spring. And a solid dim stink had moved in.

After several minutes of thinking it over he gave in to the old part of his brain, the primal core that recognised the odour in a fraction of a second. It was the sweet cloying smell of meat and it was being massaged in the unventilated warmth of the apartment. This was the last thing he expected. The air was thick with it now. Unmistakable, exposed and rank. He could not turn and flee or pretend ignorance. It was too late, he had been transformed from sleuth into witness.

The wind outside moaned and blustered against this hermetic enclosure. All the rooms around him were waiting, without tension; waiting languidly for him to soak up their lurid greed. They wanted him to find disgust in them and be done with it.

He turned his head and sniffed cautiously, trying to find a direction, an origin of that which demanded his presence, while at the same time keep the horror of imagined rotting bodies out of his head. He then moved towards the kitchen, imagining the scent more fluent there. His feet never sounded on the carpets as he passed through the corridor, into the pale dining room and then through the rubber-hinged doors. The fridge cleared its throat as he entered and shuddered some little glasses on the hard sink. The chairs seemed oddly arranged and recent, and tiny patches hooked his eyes on blots of what had surely been bright blood. He had braced himself for much worse, and now guessed that pools and puddles were elsewhere. He glided through the room, his eyes darting to check for potential attack. But deep down he knew they were not in this kitchen. He touched the cotton-wool blooms of red and saw finger marks and smears around the table. Nothing here had resulted from the preparation of food. This was an entirely different bleeding. He wanted to call out to the girl, to believe that she was still alive, maybe injured or maimed but still alive. He tried to breathe her in, sieving each molecule for a tinge of her until the swollen and bruised oxygen around him began to suffocate.

He coughed, and the sound of it touched every corner of the apartment; a sharp interior noise whose dimension and weight was in total opposition to the soft moaning of the wind outside.

The cough lasted longest in the case of the tall hall clock, hanging between the exhausted weights, the static pendulum and the anticipation of the coiled wire chime.

He moved through all the rooms, fingering the furniture and opening cupboards and wardrobes, and finding nothing. Yet the smell seemed to be getting stronger. He was horrified to find some of her night clothing in the wretched grimness of the old man's bedroom. It provoked pictures and loose movements to coat the back of his eyes. Moments of their imagined coupling gouged and churned. Pedric had unwittingly gripped one of the uprights of the iron bed frame to steady himself, then recoiled from its tacit participation. The action accelerated his exit from the room and aided his arrival at a closed door at the end of the corridor. It had to be hers. The high scent of rotting flesh was stronger than before and he wondered at his own purpose in opening it, rather than deciding to leave this terrible place forever. But the twilight was gentle and he had prepared himself for the worst.

He strode across the room with his fingers over his nostrils and pulled back the long stiff curtains. The movement of the trees thrashing in the wind outside contrasted with the sullen, static weight of the interior, and for a few seconds he marvelled at it. Then he turned to confront his worst expectations. On this side of the room near the bed the stink was unrelenting. His raw watering eyes found the smell at the centre of the offence, and he defiantly stared back at it. Nothing was there. Nobody. No body. He focused more carefully and found a bowl, a small bowl of black rancid meat paste.

'This! Only this!' he said out loud.

He looked under the bed to be sure and found even less. Close to the stinking bowl he read a name, industrially printed along its edge: 'KITTY'. It said 'KITTY'. He sat heavily on the bed.

It was almost dark when he gathered himself, the emptiness of the apartment stirring his need to leave. He stood and slowly circumnavigated the bed, without a single thought of her entering his head. Then, without any real purpose, he grabbed the lip of the sheet and gently pulled it back. The last exposure; the ultimate declaration of absence. Lying before him in a curled sleep was her shadow, unmoving and faint in the shallow light. He became thrilled and lent closer. It was barely there, a delicate remaining trace of her. He extended his hand to touch its impossibility, just once, knowing that he would disperse the spectre forever. His fingers entered its shade and it twitched. He watched amazed as a minute shudder moved through it. Then it insinuated itself over his fingers, across his hands and up his arm, a stream of it leaping towards him. His first recoil was not enough. The shock kept him in place while the 'shadow' overwhelmed him. Then it bit, or rather punctured, his understanding and sent him running back towards the landing door. The gritty dark brown tide had moved all over him and was ferociously seeking the warmth of his blood. It had been starved for days, all nutrition denied it. So it, or rather they, had sought the next best thing to blood. Warmth.

He realised they must have adhered to the last remnant of the departed child. Clustering into her thermal signature, laying in torpor in the draining heat impression of her body during her last night in the bed. They were fleas. Thousands of them. And now the ravenous infestation had a new donor to seethe upon.

SEPIA

Celeste noticed a clammy chill about Lawrence when he returned, and put this down to his overindulgence in tobacco. He seated himself beside her, adjusting his collar and cuffs, patting down any irregularities in the brilliantine of his flattened hair.

'How much longer will it be before our next pause in the journey?' she asked.

'God knows!' he spat back with a vehemence that was out of place.

She put her hand on his to comfort him in his agitated condition, but he snatched it away. And in that movement he dislodged a fraction of something that he had brought back with him from the darkness. It might have been an odour trapped in a crease of his clothing. Or perhaps even the lack of temperature of the door that still lingered near his hands. Or an inflection of the weird admiration that he had bestowed on the owners of that locked, cold room. But whatever it was had found a receptor in Celeste's straining understanding, and a bile of dread curdled her stomach and made her heart stop for a beat or two. Then her ears cleared and she heard the world differently again. The first time was when she was attacked in Au Metro and the madman tore her face apart with broken glass. She thought it must be the terror: the shock and the pain that gave her a burst of clarity; a depth of hearing that she never had before. But it didn't last, her sobs reduced within an hour to her normal level. And now it returned. She turned her head from side to side and found that her listening was pulling her through the train as if to seek an answer to its origin. She then knew there was something nearby on the train that possessed kinship with the horror of that day in the bar: the day that Lawrence had saved her while her attacker made his escape. A surge of memory engulfed her and she was hearing the voice of the other man, the stranger with black eyes, the demon who had laughed and whispered Greek words in her ear, words that were the first things to be brightened in her fleeting audible intensity and the hallucination that accompanied it.

'Vα Τον.'

'Be Him.'

As the pain of the broken glass had sheared her mouth and teeth. There was blood all over, colour before pain, as she had become the man who was stabbing her.

Suddenly, the red was splashing out, she was fleeing from her own eyes, staring at her own face as it fell apart. She was inside his skeleton composed of sorrow and guilt, then thinned to brittle anger. This gnarled masculine adrenalin hurt more that her ruined face. Every cell of this man's ghost was poisoning her, rubbing her away. She was becoming less than a cobweb. The horror and woe of it sent out a great sob, which rose up and its sound was the clearest thing she had ever heard until the demon called Tyre shouted:

'επιστρέφ.'

'RETURN.'

And she had spun back into the shaking female body and expanded as yet another gout of blood sang out of her ripped face. Firmer hands had suddenly held her.

Tyre was gone, swallowed up in the circus of whistles and shouting. The rag that she used to mop the tables was brutally applied to her face. The wrath it brought up in her was softened by another man's voice. Another command.

'Don't struggle,' it said as her panic blacked out into collapse.

Lawrence held her pinned to his chest with one arm, the other holding the rag to stop her blood and hold her face together.

'Help, please!' he called out as her weight became sudden and total. Bo Bo rushed to the side of his injured colleague and friend. This strange *pietà* found its way to the sticky floor of the bar as the room hushed and the distant hue and cry was swallowed into the white streets. Later she was hardly aware of the hospital and the stitching. Her numb, morphined mind was being tugged and nibbled. Days passed before she could speak or even think about asking for a mirror to see what she had become. How could she ever explain the nightmare of her soul entering the man who had attacked her? The memory of that nightmare had survived all the sedation . . .

How could she talk about the division of her consciousness? About her entry into the body of the hateful criminal as he fled into the snow? She had known the taste of another adrenalin, of masculine rage and defeat, of gonad, spunk and beard. The stink of fox, the phlegmed glut of violence and the relief of return to her womanhood. The hospital staff and visitors told her she was safe and healing. But the horror of being that man, even for a moment, would not go away. It was inside her, the musk of its atrocity sewn in under the sutures; a twitching miracle of evil enfolded deep into the scar of her recovery.

Lawrence had been carefully watching her and saw she had entered another state of anguish.

'Celeste! Celeste are you in pain?'

She cautiously focused on him, her head thundering and her eyes far too alive.

'Yes, my medicine please.'

'But you have had more than your daily dose already.'

'More, I need more.'

'But I told the doctors that I would control your doses.'

'I need more.'

Reluctantly Lawrence retrieved the music satchel from its hiding place in the rack above her head: flipped open the metal rod and delved into its interior, where he had taken command of her passport, other identity papers and her medications. They snuggled next to his and the deed and keys to his mother's house, along with a substantial amount of money he had removed from one of her closed accounts. He carefully unscrewed the bottle and removed one of the oval lozenges. He then folded everything back and closed the satchel tightly against further trespass. Celeste snatched at the pill and devoured it quickly, gulping it down with a hearty swig of brandy from the silver pocket flask that she carried in her bag.

Lawrence disapproved of such vulgarity. He knew it was going to take longer to help her into a more civilised world. The solitude and peace of Linay was what she needed. It would cleanse her of her tawdry past and shape her into an ideal companion. He had brought enough sedatives to keep her calm for more than a year.

He had told her they were taking a short holiday together in his home in the country, where she might recuperate and become stronger again. She had eventually agreed to his kind generosity. But she had no idea that he never intended on letting her return to her home in the city. He would cleanse her of piteous former life and her disgraceful employment in Au Metro. The savage attack which removed her beauty and erased her confidence, had purchased his leverage and secured his longing. His *kindness* and new wealth became the instrumentation of its power, and the isolation of Linay would separate Celeste from the outside world.

Lawrence would have also disapproved of the laudanum that heavily laced her brandy. But she knew her needs and that he did not have to confront them. The mixture of drugs and alcohol absorbed her fear and replaced it with a lethargy that was fathoms deep and totally without care. Now it also deadened her need to listen through the train for something that she knew to be far too close.

The scarf fell away from her face and one of the children pointed, grabbing his father's hand. Lawrence reached across her and replaced it over her now distasteful deep breathing. He also twisted her so that she slumped against him, her breast touching his immaculate shirt. It looked like affection and trust to all who might have seen it. With his free hand he extracted his pocket watch and glanced at its tyrannical pleasure. He estimated that they would be in Charleville-Mézières some time within the next two hours. They would change onto the local train there and shuffle back into the sanctity of Linay. Would she be well enough to walk? The extra pill seemed to have sapped all her energy. He might have to carry her off the train. He felt her weight against his arm and looked around the compartment at all the other luggage they had brought with them. Yes, he could do this, he was nearly there. The sunlight was glorious around them as he looked at her closed eyes, closing his own to join her for a short moment in contemplation. But he did not see the speed of her swollen orbs darting under her lids. Did not see the pressure of vision slithering against the containment of skin.

The train began to slow two miles outside of the city. Lawrence began to gather the bags from the racks above their heads and stack them by their feet. So many bags! So many prisons.

Celeste was unresponsive and he decided to decant her last. The long platforms of Gare de Charleville-Mézières began to slide alongside the train, and Lawrence with growing excitement, began to shuffle the bags into the corridor next to the exterior door. He tucked his sacred satchel tight under his arm and held it there with great pressure as he toiled with the other bags, making him look like a man suffering from a one-sided palsy or partial stroke.

Long loud jets of steam were being vented from exhausts by the engine's wheels. Their violent energy stayed low for a second or two before being wafted up into gentler clouds of disappearing vapour. The departing passengers, still with the movement of the train inside them, walked through these vanishing clouds to find the more solid domain of the entrance hall and the streets outside.

On his last run in to collect Celeste he knew he would need the strength of both arms and decided it was safe to hide the precious music satchel deep between the other bags. He would never be more than a few feet away from it at any time, and most of the other travellers flowing along the platform gave his hectic toil a wide berth. No one would ever imagine such a valuable thing would be hidden so.

He grabbed Celeste up in a determined and brutal snatch, with none of the love and care he had demonstrated before. Even some of the people in the compartment flinched at his new and unsuspected husbandry. He dragged her out into the corridor, taking her folded weight across his joined arms. Midway, her scarf, his gift, wafted from her face letting the cold exterior wind finger her wounds as the newly installed tannoy squawked the arrival of his long-awaited train now on track 6. Lawrence and his rag doll and all their luggage were on track 1. He needed a porter quickly. Celeste was barely taking her weight on her soft and buckling legs. He was no longer capable of puppeteering her and their time was running out. He let her down on the hill of piled bags, carefully guiding her weight over the secluded satchel. Then he let her crumple, and arranged her draped body in such a way that she would squarely be containing everything. He stood away from her, wiped his sweating forehead with the sleeve of his coat and looked around. The bulk of passengers had thinned and there was no sign of a porter anywhere. He looked back to the Celeste heap again and made two final adjustments. He turned her hands inward, so that they did not give her

slumped posture a look of abandonment, illness or collapse. He
also turned her head inwards and pulled up her coat collar to
conceal the shrillness of the disfigurement. He examined his
handiwork and was pleased, then turned and rushed towards the
station's entrance hall.

More announcements about arrivals and departures scratched
and mangled the air.

The train they needed would be leaving in eight minutes.
Lawrence looked at his wristwatch; sweat had misted the face of
its diminishing time. Charleville-Mézières was not a grandiose
station, but it did boast six platforms and a solid bourgeoisie
elegance required for a town of its importance and wealth.
However, its poise and immaculate cleanliness had been achieved
by a fastidious staff that had obviously long since departed. There
was a singular lack of uniformed servants everywhere, the only
exception being the one static face caged and glassed behind the
ticket window. An elderly couple was just about to engage with
this sole occupant, when Lawrence pushed them aside to enquire
at the window about his need for urgent porterage. The bored
ticket man could barely be bothered to register such urgency and
he pulled a lopsided and troubled face. The enraged spindly wife
of the displaced couple nagged and cajoled her husband to stand
up for their rights, which after a few moments he suddenly did,
squaring up between Lawrence and the indifferent window and
demanding that it was his place. The hooded eyes behind the
glass showed a glimmer of snarled joy. Lawrence could not
believe that this stupidity was blocking his plans. He tried to
sweep the old man aside saying, 'I only have one question.'

But the outraged man dug in tight.

'MY PLACE,' he bellowed into Lawrence's face.

His wife moved to his heroic side and gripped his trembling
arm.

With one stiff punch Lawrence knocked the wind out of his

bony ribs and was just about to bring his knee up into the face of the buckling old man, when a shrill whistle of steam scolded all sounds, and the teller behind the glass guillotined the shutter of his window down with great force. The first sentence of the next tannoy speech was erased by the whistle and confused by the assaulted old man's sobbing and his wife's shouting for the police. Lawrence ran back along the tracks. On his way he saw a large empty luggage truck skulking in the shadows of one of the most ornate parts of the entrance hall. Beyond it he saw the train he had just left shunt its way out of the station. He heaved the squeaking trolley from its corner and towards the exit door. Its unwieldiness seemed to be increasing as the sleek carriages departed in the opposite direction with an acceleration that was trying to shake off focus. It had left the platform, gathering speed towards Paris and the last of its hasty white steam was lifting past his eyes when he saw his target ahead: the island of bags that should have been decorated with the prone body of his Celeste. But she was not there. He swore and pushed the truck forward into a greater and greater momentum of disbelief.

She was gone, disappeared. He put his hand on the top suitcase as if feeling for residue of her warmth, or some sign that she had ever existed at all. In a leaden moment of realisation he knew that she must have got back on the train. The train that would not stop again before it reached the City of Light. A great mourning swept over him, a tragic loss; not for the woman, but for his loss of power. This mourning nearly devoured him, until it tautened and twisted into blind rage when his wandering hand found that the tan leather satchel had also disappeared.

In the train's cold compartment all was still. Mia was lying on her bunk with the cat in her lap. Aalbert was sitting in the chair re-reading a letter that had followed the last telephone call about this departure. It detailed all that was expected of him and the payment that he was due on its completion. There were also maps of Paris and directions for their journey to the hospital. Occasionally he would dart a glance at the detestable cat to be sure that it was keeping its distance. He had kept clear of the beast since his total failure at killing it. He had convinced himself that his lack of strength and the uncanny solidity of the cat's tiny body must be some kind of terrible hallucination, or a malady that he put down to emotional exhaustion, bad liquor or some species of scrofulous bane carried by the offending animal . When he had recovered from the disturbing effect the beast possessed and its power over him, he insisted that Mia and the cat be confined to her room, where they slept and ate the same mush of meat from separate bowls. He moved away from them when the water closet was used and put the trays of teeth outside the shut door. He had no intention of willingly sharing space with them again and even used a thicker glass to listen to their sounds together through the walls and the door. By the time the weather changed, and he was ordered to finally make the journey, the child and the cat had in some strange way become one.

All the while Aalbert fantasised more and more horrible ways to kill the cat.

Now the animal seemed to sense his speculation and glared at him from under Mia's hands as the train gently rocked them towards Paris.

Aalbert returned to his papers and to calculate his forthcoming payment. Again he began to speculate on what he would spend it on, over the following years. His concentration was occasionally flinched by a tiny high click in the compartment, and his wrinkled eyes flicked up at each dry chime, looking and seeing nothing, then returning to the paper, absorbed in its minute detail. The clicks found sympathy and timing with the commas and full stops of the tight black ink on the page. The whistle of the train shrieked and a small jolt made him fold the letter away.

The chill of the room was beginning to affect him, and he collected a woollen jacket and draped it about his shoulders. Maybe it was best just to doze through the next few hours, before he managed to get paid and escape. He looked at the child stroking and fingering the detestable cat, and saw her seek deeper into the fur of its neck, probing quietly with an absent-minded intensity he had seen somewhere before. She paused and found something in the cat's fur that she then brought up to her face. She briefly examined her pinched fingertips with great concentration, before putting them into her mouth, a second after the click sounded again. What was she doing? He pretended not to watch. When she did it again he remembered where he had seen the exact action before. It was in 'De Zoologie' in Antwerp, in the monkey house. She was grooming and preening the cat in exactly the same ways that monkeys do. The tiny insistent clicking that he had been hearing for hours was her splitting the carapace of a flea. Mia was biting the detestable insect between her teeth of ice and glass, and enjoying the consequences.

GREEN

Celeste had somehow returned to her original seat on the train before she passed out and was in a deep, unnatural sleep whose thick broth of images and sounds were all contradictory, brutal and puerile.

When she awoke, she was alone in the rocking sunlight of the empty compartment. The other two remaining passengers had quietly moved elsewhere. Celeste tried to recall all that had happened and piece the troubled sticky memories together: where was Lawrence? Suddenly she heard a tiny click, like the cocking of a miniature pistol. It repeated again and again and it instantly unblocked her amnesia. She was back on the pile of bags, on the hard platform alone. Coming to, finding herself abandoned outside the train.

She remembered her eyes opening. Trying to sit up, but a dark bone-chilling cold had leached the action, sending her sideways, scattering the piled suitcases in different directions. Her scarf was gone and one hand covered her face while the other spidered across the surface of the bulk of the suitcases, trying to find purchase, support or meaning, a grip of reality. Her hand suddenly touched something different. She looked down; her fingers were lightly hooked onto the cold brass of the music satchel containing her pills, her passport and her life. She ferociously snatched it up and the act changed her eyes and erected the adrenalin that turned her towards the train. And knew that she had to get back on, to complete a journey that she did not understand. She had heard the clicking and it made her rush to get on the train.

Then she had seen the flash of green, the vivid tongue of her scarf trapped in the closed carriage door. Its hopeless injury had turned into a beacon and she stumbled towards it, staggering to the door, grabbing the thick metal handle, and wrenching it open with all her strength. A terrible shrill scream sounded somewhere above her and she felt a lurch shudder through all that was solid. The great weight of the door swung open and twisted her balance, and as the train lurched into movement one of her legs slid between the train and the lip of the platform. She threw the satchel inside and flailed and clawed her way back in, her legs kicking the air as she tried to gain purchase. She swam, crawled and propelled her sprawling face down the corridor as the train shunted out of the station.

Someone on the platform had slammed the door shut on the clouds of steam. One of her shoes had fallen off and was lost forever, and she was covered in grime. She sobbed. She had reached safety. But why? What was on this train that she so needed? She looked down at her bruised and filthy hands, one grabbing the scarf; some of the fingernails were broken. Gradually she got to her feet as the train gathered speed and began to leave Charleville-Mézières behind as a memory of confusion. She picked up Lawrence's satchel. Lawrence! Where was Lawrence?

She had looked down the twisting length of the train's corridors. Then her pain had reminded her why she had saved the satchel; it contained her pills, the knowledge of which gave her the strength and determination to find her seat and the promise of rest. This took some time because they all looked the same and the family that they had shared the compartment with before were gone and so was all of her and Lawrence's luggage. The shock of that was unimportant compared to her need for the pills. She had opened the sliding door of the first empty compartment and wedged herself into the seat nearest the window. She then dug deep into satchel and retrieved the pills, swallowing two and washing them into the desired bliss with a long gulp of laced brandy from her hip flask. She touched her face and felt again the reassuring smoothness of the scarf.

While waiting for the effects to take her she had looked at the other contents of his prized possession. Squeezed into its intimate confinement she found their passports and some legal papers tied in ribbon, three chinking heavy keys and an envelope bursting with bank notes.

It was then she had realised that Lawrence was truly gone; he had been left behind on that station whose name she did not know and she had all the papers and legal chattels that he had talked about with such vigour and excitement. She had the keys to his home. She had resolved to leave the train at the next station and return to find him . . . but where?

His house was in a small village near the station where they had been separated. Its name would be somewhere within those papers. She had pulled all the documents out of the satchel, laying them on the empty seats. She separated the train tickets for their obvious immediate use, and in doing so was surprised to see that he had bought only singles. A one-way journey?

She had been puzzling on this when she turned over a slim technical folder with a green string holding it closed. Her name was written into the subject box on the front cover. She left the rest and opened it to discover what was within its pages. It contained mainly hospital reports and receipts for treatment. It was clear that he had paid them all. His kindness took her breath away again. She had read deeper into the file, past her injured face into blood tests and concerns that she did not recognise. Her memory of her treatment was vague and hazy, centred on her obvious wounds, but she was aware of having other examinations that she wondered about.

Some had been intimate and uncomfortable, but she did not resist or even ask their purpose. Suddenly here were the results of such prying, and the shock twisted something inside her. The papers said that she was free from infections and listed all those that had been searched for. The usual ones like TB were there. The kindness was beginning to have a prying edge. The next page listed every known venereal disease, a few of which she had never heard of. Her stomach turned and she returned to the covering letter that she had only skim-read before. There it was in black and white: Lawrence had paid for those tests to be performed, and the results were his property alone. Her body had been systematically assessed in a process of medical violation so that this man could be sure that his new possession was not flawed or contaminated in any possible way.

Small parts of her mind had not been able to accept this sickening fact and they scurried around the evidence trying to find another, more innocent conclusion. But no matter how much they contoured and shoved, no other explanation fitted the template with such perfect conviction. For what could have been a minute or a day she had sat rigid in a calcification of shock and nausea. The warm countryside rushed past the train's windows and all her plans charred, and her hope and gentleness collapsed into an incineration of quicklime, a citric dust as sharp as glass and determined as mercury. In that short time she had become somebody else, so that when her red eyes found the papers again, their hunger inverted all her previous purpose. She had removed the money, her passport and her ticket, and put her medical reports back in the satchel with his passport, the keys and deeds of the house, and many other vital securities. She looped the handle through the metal bar and pulled it tight; exactly at that moment there had been a dramatic change in the rhythmic sound of the train as the first effects of the drugs and alcohol had rippled through her. She stood up and went to the outer door that she had struggled with. Its window was still open, and a wide vista of water shone far below. The black iron struts of the long bridge they were crossing shudder-danced to match the change in the pitch of the rails, and in perfect timing with them she had thrown the music satchel spinning out into the wide, bright space of emphatic emptiness and the deep waters below.

Five

UMBER

*T*here is a great irony in Paris being called the City of Light. The clarity of that naming from the Enlightenment was later extinguished with the blood and shouting of The Terror. Even the illumination of the Champs-Élysées by gas lamps in 1828 was too late to drive away the sulking shadows that engulf the twenty arrondissements with a sinister and concealing stealth. Compare its midnight atmosphere in any season with other major European cities and feel the contrasts. There is nothing of the innocence of Amsterdam or the surprising and defiant majesty of Berlin. And London's vast indifference with its cherished highlights of obvious criminality seems vague and elderly in comparison. The only other major European capital that shivers in its past and still breathes darkness is Rome. One feature they both uniquely share is being honeycombed with the dead. Catacombs wind beneath the glittering boulevards and under the formality of ornate gardens. In a more intimate manner, the same weight of active shadow can be found in Edinburgh, although it is not the bodies of the dead that dwell in that underground city.

The being who shared his name with the King of Tyre had residencies IN ALL THREE.

Even in this hour of Parisian mid-morning there is a presence that broods in the gaiety and bustle: an ominous watching in the waiting. Railway stations are prodigious resonators for this phenomenon, and the Gare du Nord is a cathedral to such strangeness. A restless hunger inhabits the swirling opalescence of noise and steam high in its iron and glass ribcage. The constant respiration of humans through the lungs of arrival and departure, a tidal ocean of bodies and souls; their dreams and fears, longings and dreads all heightened by the expectation or exhaustion of journey.

Celeste's train shuddered along one of the many iron arteries into the heart of the city.

It had been a bad night for her. No solace could now be found in any part of her scurrying mind. The drugs had offered no white pocket for her anxieties to nest in. She had been swindled of repose and the closedown of her rioting emotions. All her receptacles of mind and soul still bristled or burnt with unrelenting spiteful chatter, which was now matched by the squealing of iron wheels and the lurches of rail track points as they orchestrated her arrival. The city began to swallow the train.

Then, without any species of warning, it all stopped. A darkness closed her in and something like her previously desired unconsciousness enveloped her. Something like sleep, deep and imageless sleep, swallowed her, the sweetness of its balm swaddling her into rest. This had happened before, long before when she was young. It had happened with the man who had given her Oskar, her poor son. That wonderful man who had told her so much and treated her like a woman when in truth she was still a child. He had been sixty-five years old and going blind, a guest at the great house where she was a maid. It was an old story that everybody thought they knew; the seduction of the meek by the powerful. But it had never been like that.

Dr Axel was different to any man she had ever met before or since, and it had been her giving, her insistence that brought Oskar into the world: a world that she had never experienced before she spoke to him. In those few weeks he had told her of so many wonderful things; stories of lights, warmth and hugeness. Stories of ghosts in sun-flooded gardens of Roman emperors, of the cruelties of medicine, of the love and conversations of animals. Of mountains and palaces of snow. Forests of mist that froze, clinging to the trees like glass, becoming ice chandeliers that might be played with sticks, like dulcimers, under the shifting colours of the aurora borealis. He gave her things to stop the mind's drudgery, and make it grow. Her little gift of her trembling body was so small compared to the universe he bestowed on her and the generosity of his belief in her understanding. He had also enchanted her with a sensation of the living dream, that he called 'hipgnosis', and it had removed a fear that she had carried since childhood. He had explained how 'hipgnosis' could be a tool for good or evil. The sensation it gave her soothed away so much dread that she believed it could only come from God.

But now she realised that it had left an aperture in her that had never really closed, and the lips of it tasted the sense of disembodiment that had occurred in her violation in Au Metro. And with the turning of this key of revelation, she knew that some part of her fled herself and found a place in that vicious assailant, and that was what she was sharing and hearing. Grit filled her veins as she again tasted his sickening pungency.

Further down the train in the first-class compartment, Aalbert choked out of a disturbing sleep, in a trembling fit that scared Mia, who had been putting the cat gently into its portable cage. The train slowed a half-mile from the station and all the other passengers started preparing to leave. A general bustle filled the carriages and everyone began to talk. The whistles of other trains could be heard. By the time the great glass roof slid over them and the train prepared to pant out its last breath, everybody on board was standing ready to leave, except for the Earwig, Mia and Celeste. Aalbert was in shock, knowing that somebody close by was observing him. His dream had told him that all his secrets had been trespassed upon, all his guilt tasted. Mia pulled on his long bony fingers. She was shouting agitated and mangled words through a splutter of ice and a splinter of glass. When the train finally stopped, he violently shrugged off his fear and snatched up the child and their luggage and she grabbed the caged cat and fled the cool chamber into the heat and size of the great station. Then they joined the tide of passengers. Somewhere near the seventh carriage, Mia turned to look back at the train and saw the woman in the green scarf staring out of the train window at them. Her eyes, like the cat's, did not blink.

Celeste had left her seat and was standing in the corridor, her face pressed close to the glass of the door, staring out onto the platform. One of the porters spotted her long after the other passengers had departed. He was used to sleepers and drunks overstaying their journey, but realised instantly that she was neither of those.

Only her eyes could be seen; the rest of her face was hidden, wrapped tightly in some kind of green garment. The expression in her eyes was unrecognisable, but of such an intensity that even when viewed from ten metres away and through the glass of the carriage door it was overwhelming. He cautiously approached and opened it slowly. She looked straight through him and seemed fixed on one spot on the platform behind him.

'Madame, this is the end of the journey. You have arrived in Paris, and this train goes no further.'

He knew his words were worthless to her, but needed their prosaic certainty for his own comfort, the truth being that the look of this woman was beginning to unnerve him.

'Are you all right, madame? May I help you disembark?'

Her eyes flickered slightly, and a little of the porter's presence was allowed through into her awareness. Then she whispered muffled green words from under the tight scarf.

'Did you . . . did you see *him*?'

As the porter tried to understand the words her eyes pointed at a place behind his straining face. 'Out there, *he* was out there with a child.'

She now knew why she had got back on the train. Because he had been on it too. The monster who deformed her body and contaminated part of her soul had been only a few carriages away and now he had stolen a child!

The Hotel Terminus Nord was opposite the gigantic facade of Gare du Nord and intended to have its own say about grandeur. The porter who ferried the shabby luggage of these peculiar passengers across the frantic road to the hotel had no opinion about how they looked. He resolutely ignored the taciturn stiffness of the old man who pulled the girl along on a tight leash. And he did not notice that she and the cat she carried in a basket had matching looks of shock as if their eyes might fall out.

The wardens at reception were expecting them; or rather a normal version of what they were told would occupy one of their 'nicest rooms'. They hastily ushered them to it on the first floor without a word of enquiry or complaint being proffered about the cat, whose cries scratched against the white marbled perfection of the lobby, the gilt interior of the lift and the endless corridors of muffled secrets.

Another porter escorted Celeste to the same chaos of traffic outside the station, and told her that there were many pensions and bars with rooms nearby. He then beat a hasty retreat back into the station. No sensible plan occurred to her as she stood staring around, other than to get far away from the station by the time Lawrence arrived. Even though in her heart of hearts she knew he would never come, she used the fear of it to drive her diagonally across the thundering road and into the long tall alleys of the old city.

Eventually she stopped outside a small bar that smelt like Au Metro. She regained her control in one of its darkest corners with the aid of two brandies and one of the pills that she had saved from the satchel. An ancient stair led up from the bar to four small bedrooms. She paid in folded cash and took a third brandy with her into a locked snug little room that did not jolt or smell of cinders, children or crime. With the strength she had left she vowed that she would find this terrible old man, who refused to go away and insisted not only on haunting her fetid dreams, but also on actually existing and travelling beside her. She must confront his audacity and challenge him, as the only enemy she had ever had. She would track him like game and finish this once and for all. Then, exhausted, she looked into her cups, finding only out-of-focus ghosts of her plans. She prayed to her glass for a dreamless sleep, which was granted the moment her head touched the clean but well-used pillow.

Mia could or would not rest. Once she had roamed and explored every inch of room 103, she started again. The cat followed her on the first two circuits, but gave up on the third and retired to the girl's bed. There was nothing in the controlled luxury to amuse her and she sensed the bleakness bluntly shining beneath the ornate.

She picked at her mouth and poked at the cat and watched Aalbert savouring his brandy. He was different in a way she did not understand. This was going to be their last night together and excitement sizzled under his pasty stiff drunkenness. His job was done and the promised payoff was going to be generous, and would ensure his freedom for at least the next couple of years. He would leave the City of Light rich and foot-free; a condition that he had never really experienced before.

He absently gazed at the strange child and tried for the last time to understand what was happening behind those limpid but emphatic eyes. He had had enough of her and the prospect of her continual growth rubbed up a mild disgust in him. Best to never think of the woman that she would become. Best to forget this singular passage of his life and rinse it out of the grey cabinets in his skull. Then she said: 'Unku.'

AMBER

*H*ow was she going to find him in a city of this size and complexity? Where would she start? Celeste sat in the bar of the snug hotel, deflated and feeling foolish at the stupidity of her quest. Its clarity had been born in bright daylight, and now she was thinking about going home. She absent-mindedly retraced her steps back to the station. Then she remembered the child.

What would an odious villain like that be doing with a child? He looked too old to be its father and no woman would ever place a grandchild in the care of such a man. Had he stolen her? Such a crime would not be out of place. She allowed herself for the first time to ponder on the images and senses that had so devastated her before.

Because of the plight of the child, she tasted every trace of the horror. Her recent thoughts of Dr Axel had also continued, and many of the things he had told her flooded back into a mind that was now old enough to understand them. Perhaps it was because she was in Paris, the city of his youth, where so many of his most vivid stories took place, especially the ones of the mind and how he learnt how it worked. Difficult things to understand, but he always tried to find a way to explain. He had told her that memory and imagination are processes of the mind that share a close tie and a similarity that is difficult to separate. One of the more eloquent explanations he used suggested that it might be a difference in emphasis, the depth of impression, and he used the image of footprints in the snow to illustrate it. The print of memory, he said, might be heavier than that of imagination. But what occurs in the same snow field when recollection is consciously released and encouraged to retrace the tracks of a recent vivid memory? What is the impression when imagination and memory share the same shoe? And which guides which?

Celeste had started this path on tiptoe when a taint or an echo of another memory showed itself. It was calling to her and for the first time she did not shiver and recoil from it. With trepidation she strained to listen, now knowing that she would find him through her ears.

Aalbert had ordered food to be brought to their room. He could not face the repellent mixture of embarrassment and stultifying politeness that always graces hotel restaurants. And with Mia as a dining companion a thousand other unknown possibilities of outrage and humiliation could be guaranteed. So dinner was brought to them and eaten at a small rectangular table of over-polished wood, fragile and turned bitter in its varnish, with the room service trolley parked tightly against it. This little convenience had caused some agitated disagreement between the Earwig and the tight little waiter. Aalbert knew the ways of such lowly servants and had no intention of feeding the ferocity of below-stairs tongues, so had hidden Mia in the bathroom with the cat.

'Just leave the trolley. When I am finished I will put it outside.'

'Outside, sir?'

'When I am finished.'

'But I must take the trolley with me, sir.'

'No, leave it.'

'After I have served.'

'No, just leave it.'

'But, sir—'

'Leave it.'

And with his last word on the matter Aalbert rudely pointed at the door. The waiter gathered himself, curtly nodded and left. Nothing more would be ordered from the hotel. Aalbert knew the tip-less, insulted waiter was planning little unsavoury extras to be added to 'Sir's' next order from the kitchen or the bar. Aalbert was far too cunning to become victim to such malicious pranks. He knew what they were because he had practised many himself over the years. By dismissing the waiter, he had also relieved himself of the smirking contempt with which the waiter would be reacting to his peculiar choice of foods – boiled plaice and porridge sitting opposite lamb cutlets and foie gras, tepid milk and claret. He might even have enquired about the purpose of the extra serviettes and napkins that he had ordered with the meal.

After he had laid out the food and mixed the porridge with the fish he retrieved the child and cat from the bathroom and set Mia at the table. Her small chewing head looked like the cat's as they both watched him devour the lamb. The napkins had been tucked in around the girl's neck and shoulders, turning them into bibs to protect her from spillage. The cat had moved to beneath the hanging cloth in anticipation of the soggy avalanche that would fall into its toothless appetite. It was a queer still moment, the concentration on the food giving off a quietness that mimicked domestic normality; almost a family.

Celeste knew there was no going back. She was in her tiny room above the bar and she knew, too, what to do. Some part of her had changed and a tendril of vengeance had swollen into a tentacle of revenge. So she would make an audible mirror to scry for any futures and seek them on the other side of a reflection of oblivion. She set it out on the small bedside table; it was made of drink and drugs. At twilight she began to apply its layers behind the transparent woman she had always been.

VIOLET

It had been almost forty years since Charcot had died, but his stern Napoleonic ghost still haunted the wards and treatment rooms of the great hospital. The ghost had tutted and shaken his gnome-like head at the squabbling politics that threatened to undermine all he had created at Salpêtrière. The hysteria and mania of the patients was nothing compared to the neurosis, paranoia and envy among the staff. From the moment that he had left, everything began to fall apart. But somehow the reputation of the clinic of the mind survived.

Perhaps the vivid energy of his teachings had embedded itself in the fabric of the buildings. Young practitioners flocked to Salpêtrière; new theories of treatment found a home. And after the ravages of the Great War there was no shortage of material to work with or on. Indeed a new wing was even now being built over the gardens where the great man had insisted that his female 'circus' must take their daily air and compulsory exposure to the weak rays of the city's sunshine.

The sound of sawing and the pulse of a piling hammer could be heard as Aalbert and Mia walked up the impressive driveway towards the main entrance of the hospital. He held her hand and she carried the cat in the basket by its squeaking handle in her other hand, a pendulum registering their pace of approach. A subdued elation made Aalbert's step almost jaunty. He tried not to rush and tug the girl forward. He was near the completion of this section of his life, and his longing for the next was becoming overwhelming. Nothing would stop him now. Even the distasteful incident at the hotel had been washed aside in his desire to sign her off, collect his money and again start anew. The cobbles beneath their feet changed tone as the solid stone of the hospital gained the ground and spoke of its proximity.

The entrance hall was high and full of the sound of activity. Mia flinched at being so close to so many fast-moving people. The Earwig gripped the flinch and pulled her closer. By the time they reached the desk signposted '*Accueil*', the animal had started making a noise that caused the Earwig to cover his ears, thus presenting the receptionist with a peculiar tableau. Fortunately such manifestations were not uncommon in and about the vicinity of Salpêtrière. With titanic calm the woman smiled icily at the child, ignored the rude old man and spoke directly to the cat. Her mewing tones instantly silenced the beast and flattened the stiff fur around its neck and spine.

There is an understanding with all domestic felines when they enter the presence of A Cat Owner, that most advanced of all the human species, who willingly shares a life, secrets and parts of the soul with a permanently disdainful house guest. The cat looked intently out of the cage, pressing its small head against the bars, and started yawning and pawing its enclosure. The keen-eyed woman, who was called Avril Dotrice, first saw the lack of teeth. And then saw the lack of claws. She had heard of such outrageous travesties being inflicted on poor defenceless creatures before. She could not bear such abominations. All her cats were kept in their most natural state, including the two toms who fought and sprayed every day. This is what gave Mademoiselle Dotrice a certain distinctive presence, no matter how much she boiled her clothing and perfumed herself before setting off to work every morning.

She decided she had never met such an odious human face to face before. She glared at Aalbert with unrestrained contempt.

'I have brought the child as requested,' he said unperturbed. 'I believe you have some papers for me to sign. Monsieur Scellinc. Monsieur Aalbert Scellinc.'

She wrenched her eyes off him and stabbed them into the one of the huge ledgers that lay open on the desk before her. Her curved fingernail found his squalid name halfway down the second column. The finger lifted vertically and moved sideways to one of a series of electric buttons that ran from the edge of the desk to different far-off departments of the hospital. Her other hand clenched into a pink spearhead that pointed to a distant bench. 'Wait there,' she commanded, without ever meeting his eyes again.

She did, however, give a worried glance at the child and an affectionate tilt towards the cat. The Earwig slouched off, dragging Mia behind him, and Mlle Dotrice retrieved the appropriate bundle of papers from one of the many pigeonholes that occupied the space behind her.

The doctor who came to meet them at the bench twenty minutes later, was very tall and even thinner than the Earwig, more a kind of stick insect. He greeted Aalbert formally but only really had eyes for Mia. After a few stiff moments he sat himself down with the child and spoke to her in crystal Parisian French. While he spoke and observed her, his body pivoted on the hard bench, turning himself away from her old guardian until he almost had his back to him. Mia did not know what to do. Nobody had ever said so many words to her before or stared so excitedly into her eyes. The few glances that Pedric had given showed an appetite, but this man was displaying an open hunger. He even bent his back to lower his gaze so that he could see inside her mouth, when it opened without words.

'She has been well cared for,' blurted Aalbert in an attempt to remind the doctor that he was still there.

'Yes I can see that, excellent.'

This was said with a distraction that was generated by concentration. The words were meant not as communication or a compliment for the old man, but just as plain fact.

'Excellent,' he said again.

Then he touched her hand as if to take her pulse and she flinched back. The doctor suddenly grabbed her hand with both of his. There was a brutality in it that she had never experienced, and it made her soften.

'You must not be afraid, my dear, you are safe here with us.'

She had no idea what he meant. In her limited life every other thing except the cat had touched her through caution, duty or disgust, while the strength of this man in the white coat was like the lucidity of snow.

Aalbert saw this and shakily began to stand up.

'I . . . I think there are papers?' he mumbled with a voice that had dried away. 'Papers that I must sign.'

The doctor looked annoyed and unsure, then tightened.

'Yes, that is right. Go back to Madamoiselle Dotrice and complete them now, please.'

And with this he also stood and took Aalbert's elbow, showing him the way forward and away from them. The cat made a low growling sound in its throat as he passed. And he had the uncontrollable idea that the beast had copied the tone and vibration from the refrigerator back in the kitchen in Liège.

Celeste had reached the entrance of the great hospital and stood staring at its strange name, written in wrought iron over a gate. She knew this name. *He* had spoken it many times, before he had become a great man, in his youth when he was a medical student. She carefully pronounced the word and heard it tune itself to his voice and the stories that he had told her. How could this happen? It smelt of destiny, and she tingled as she approached.

*   *   *

The papers were laid out on a table in a small room behind the *Accueil* counter. Avril Dotrice was standing over them, anxious to see this task completed. Aalbert looked at the pages and read some of the words written in a curious violet ink. His name was inscribed in the same colour by the same hand on a separate envelope.

That was the money, he was sure. His mouth was parched, as if sand blown by the husk of his faltering voice. He licked his lips and took up the pen. 'Where?' he asked.

The same curved nail tapped the paper in three places, turned over several sheets and tapped again. He began to scrawl his name and with each new signature gained a violent intoxication of freedom and wealth, so that his name became bigger and more flamboyantly applied as he continued. He was one signature away from escape when Mlle Dotrice asked, 'What is the actual age of your daughter?'

He was midway through the loop of the second L when he halted.

'Age?' he said, mistakenly saying the wrong word of shock. Or saying it to avoid the other word that was growing heavy between dough and slaughter.

'Yes! What is her exact age?'

He stopped writing and allowed the true mistake to form in his mouth.

'Daughter?'

The sound, or rather the feeling, of it on his tongue was totally wrong, and he had to dredge up the other words to make sense of it.

'She is not my daughter.'

The air in the small room changed colour.

'Then why are you signing her over to us?' asked the *Accueil*.

He straightened and looked at her. Something of her hostility had changed; she was poised in a different way, her skeletal stance being overcome by muscle. This, he knew, made her far more dangerous.

'I am just her keeper, nothing more,' he said faintly.

Dotrice stepped forward and the Earwig moved aside. She was at the papers, turning the pages, slowly.

'What is her name?' she barked.

'Mia,' the Earwig barely said.

'Mia what?'

Aalbert was silent. He did not know, he had never asked. No one had ever told him.

'LOOK,' she demanded, the nail becoming a claw on the wincing paper.

He moved forward and stooped down to see. Above the gleaming curve and slightly reflected in its polished keratin was the indelibly written name of Mia Marie Scellinc.

'No,' he said. 'No.' And the knock of it became big in his mouth and in his head.

'NO.'

The white truculence of the paper had to hear it. She had to hear it. The room had to hear it. And outside in the corridor and on the wooden bench the doctor and the child, even the cat had to hear it.

'NO!' he barked. 'This is nonsense.'

He looked around him and at her. There was nothing in her eyes he cared to recognise. He looked back at the paper, his hand with the pen still in it and a flat package inscribed with his name. His name. This must be the money. He rushed at the pages of the document, turning them back against the offending lie and found the place where his signature was half-finished. He took a gulp of breath and completed it, but in a thinner, tighter style, making it look like a forgery committed by two different hands. He dropped the pen, picked up the package and left without a word. Outside on the bench only the cat in the basket remained. The child and the doctor were gone. A sibilant spiteful hissing was coming from the basket. Aalbert turned his back on it and made his way out of the looming hospital. The steam hammer and sawing had stopped.

Celeste had survived the mirror. She was trembling and deaf in one ear but her face no longer hurt. A series of spasms during the night had re-tuned her face; the exposed sinews had tightened, pulling her mouth into something that looked like an infant's drawing of a smile, or a sneer turned upside down. But the most important thing was that she now had a clarity about the Earwig. She could catch flakes of his voice in her dead ear and she would follow them into their meeting. But before that she had to go shopping. The hotel owner had told her where she might purchase the rare libation that she so insisted on. She had it with her now, a hidden gift in a brown paper bag.

She was in the central hall of Salpêtrière staring at a large picture hung high against one wall. It was a copy of André Brouillet's painting of the neurologist Jean-Martin Charcot, *Une Leçon Clinique à la Salpêtrière, 1887*. She read the title again and again. This was the very man that Dr Axel told her horror stories of. She had had no idea then what he looked like, and now she knew. She had imagined a long thin man with a pointed beard and red devil eyes, imposing and as powerful as Dr A had described. But the Charcot who dominated this picture was nothing like that, he looked like a peasant or an artisan. He was short and slightly hunched, with a broad brow, a downturned mouth and a pendulous Italian nose. Yet there was a power about him; a muscular resistance tinged with cruelty. Once she was over her surprise she searched the other faces in the painting. There were twenty or so other men in the picture intently listening to Charcot's lecture. She desperately hoped one of them might be Dr A. She longed to see his face again, even as a young man. But he was not there.

Then Celeste looked at the female patient in the picture, who was being held up by another doctor and a nurse. This was one of those that he spoke about. One of the prima donnas from the Salle St Agnes: the ward of the *grandes hysteriques*. The woman in the painting was in spasm, her arms twisted behind her back, the rest of her body limp and suggestive. It was exactly as Dr A had said: a theatre of grotesque acting and real somnambulist seizures. Staged every Tuesday for Charcot's insatiable ego, his circus of fallen women performing all manner of tremors and spasms at his command. The problem in all of this entertainment was the science, and Dr A did not believe a word of the exaggerated claims that the master of Salpêtrière made. Dr A said that half the women had only become mad with all the experiments that the young doctors had been encouraged to perform on them, layer upon layer of mesmeric suggestion, producing a sickly, toppling cake of dementia and depravity. At the time Celeste had little understanding of these things, but over the years she looked after the seeds of knowledge that the great doctor had sewn and added her own nutriments of reading and attending certain classes of Christian education. She understood that too much medicine can torture a soul, can corrupt and condemn it. The Queens of the Salle St Agnes were extravagant fakes, some flaunting imaginary symptoms to gain status and favour. Such creatures were beyond charity. Celeste was divining to which camp the woman in the painting belonged, when the Earwig hurried past her, oblivious to her presence or identity.

He was alone. He had left the child somewhere in this terrible place. He had given her up to the mercy of those who grilled sensibilities for pleasure; pulled the wings off the lowly to see how they would fly. She hurried back in the direction from which he had just fled to be sure that the child did not linger there, to be certain that she did not mistake this man. She saw the mewing cat and its cage abandoned on the lonely bench and knew that everything she had ever felt had been confirmed. Justified.

Accueil Dotrice was putting the papers away when she realised that Scellinc had not left a forwarding address. She gathered herself and rushed outside to confront him. The hall was empty. Then the cat called her from its isolation on the wooden bench.

'Poor thing,' she exclaimed and quickly retrieved it, carrying the basket back to her little office behind the desk.

The cat's jet black eyes watched her every move.

'Poor thing, you must be starving,' she muttered to herself as she retrieved a small flask of milk from her lunch box and poured some out into a cracked soup bowl.

She placed it next to the basket and opened the complicated latch. The cat slid out and purred, rubbing itself against her ankle before pushing its head into the bowl and drinking loudly.

'What am I to do with you?' she asked, knowing that the poor mutilated animal could not fend for itself in the wild but that her company of pets would also make it unwelcome.

'And what do you eat, with no teeth?' she conjectured.

And then, still talking out loud, she answered herself.

'Maybe a little bread and broth, or fish and porridge.'

She was pleased with the solution and turned to inform the cat of its future repast.

But it was gone, only a few splashes of milk around the bowl to show that it had been there at all.

PURPLE

Outside the day had changed: bright sunshine and rains quarrelling for the skies and sweeping the avenues with bold contradictions. Rainbows must be forming, and somewhere the tension of their arcs was glorifying the air above or behind the tall buildings. Aalbert turned his soaking collar up against the squalls and shaded his eyes against the intense infliction of light. White birds were being blown off course. The world around him was in a disarray of elements and celebrating every second of it.

How long had he been walking? His deep-rooted sense of survival had piloted him across streets, violent with traffic. He was in a daze and all the elements of his life were detaching and shifting as if the day's weather was rearranging them. He tried not to align dates and places in his past, because they kept settling like unruly papers on the desk of that miserable hospital clerk. The truth was that his memory refused to go back that far. How could he be expected to remember? He was so far away from that stinking war and its aftermath of poverty. He had dug new trenches in this side of that time, and they were steadfast and deep.

A cold slithered beneath his clothing that was worse than anything he had encountered in the Great White. The sounds around him had changed and he saw the trees. He was in a tall alley of trees. The street and the buildings were gone. He had found his way into the centre of the Jardin du Plantes. The wind in this tall avenue had a pulse caused by its buffeted weaving between the regular trunks. It plucked at his clothing and the package in his hand. He stared at it for a long time, then tore it open.

Inside was the letter of termination of his contract, two letters of recommendation, a banker's order for 7,000 francs and a copy of a birth certificate that he never wanted to see. An intolerable betrayal of memory was unwinding all his plans. His treacherous spine even turned as if ready to steer the rest of him back into the hospital and retrieve the child. He dug his curved shoes into the ground and into a lie. He shoved all the papers into different pockets of his clothing and gathered himself to go on. The weather was making his face wet and he wiped his eyes, refusing to acknowledge anything other than rain. The bleary greens around him condemned him. He must leave this place; get away further from the malign gravitation of the hospital and thoughts of Mia, somewhere in its core. She was alone and terrified, he was sure. But they had drugs and therapy for such things; it was no longer his business. And where was he now? He had been walking lost in speculations, tormented.

He looked around again at the avenues of tall trees that held him in their perspective. This was the truth, a little man lost in forces that he never understood. Not a monster of cruel indifference, but a puppet. He exhaled and opened his senses to all around him; tree, shrub and grass smells. Floods of green and white air licked at his dryness, and amid them Lily of the Valley becoming the most strident. He walked through it and started to gather speed, when he suddenly realised that he was rushing in the wrong direction. He slowed on the path when he heard somebody close by, approaching quickly across the gravel. One of the doctors had come to bring him back, or maybe the miserable *Accueil* was here to tell him that it had all been a mistake, that his name had never been printed against a birth. A blur was coming out of the line of trees toward him. He half turned to accept the next conditions of compromise and defeat.

It was a woman that was speeding towards him. A stranger? A friend? Perhaps it was Marie, he thought, wanting the impossible to mount the intangible and beget an answer. But it was not her. For a moment he allowed his eyes to leave her savage face and check her body for familiarity. Then he saw the distinctive neck of a bottle of Westvleteren XII clutched in her white hand. Saint Sixtus had come to Paris. He smiled in the wet breeze as time slowed and gathered thick about him, and through the distortion he clearly saw her ruined face and recognised who it was rushing towards him, and that the raised bottle was not a salutation to his triumph. Nothing was in the bottle, because the bottle wasn't there. Only its thick dark neck and a razor sharp portion of its broken shoulder were seeking his mouth, which opened without a word before it was ripped apart.

Celeste made the first stab blunt and hard, and only on its withdrawal did she tear it from side to side, giving her enough shock time to lash it back and snap the black glass into his gums and tongue again. On the third stab the Earwig screamed through his pain and shock, caught her wrist and deflected the blow. Then she wildly brought her other arm up and scratched at his eyes. But the Earwig was hard and strong, and he grabbed that arm too, pulling it down to her side to copy the containment of its twin. Her body writhed and he crushed it close, knowing that his only chance of survival was to keep her pinned thus; using all the strength of his arms to subdue her, and forcing their bodies to become one. His mistake was to underestimate the momentum of her ferocity and in an off-balance moment she rammed her head against his, her mouth biting into the broken glass that was embedded in his detached lip and gum. The Earwig was left with no defence other than attack, so he bit back and their gnawing heads embraced. Old, healed wounds opened their stitching.

New wounds flooded the broken teeth and bitten tongues in an uncontrollable exchange of passion. Only fatigue, blood loss and despair would eventually allow the kiss to subside and slow into knowledge.

From a distance, back in the shrubbery, the couple that stood locked together at the central perspective of the row of symmetrical trees appeared normal. The intimacy of their embrace was gently buffeted by the sunlit wind that wove between the tall trunks and thrashing leaves. The watcher looked for a few more seconds then turned and made its way north, out of the gardens. It was going to be a long journey home for such a lone beast, and the parks and the roads showed no sympathy or compassion for a cat. It would be an hour or so until it would reach its residence, in the sixth arrondissement in the shadow of Saint-Sulpice.

ACKNOWLEDGEMENTS

(I have only just grasped the purpose and distinction of acknowledgments; so, I must begin by thanking all those who kindly gave their time, energy and faith to every one of my previous works. Now that I have finally gained wisdom, here we go . . .)

Enormous thanks to Mia, who walked into my waking life, pointed at her mouth and told me her name.

To Geoff Cox, to whom I first shared the experience of her visitation, and who subsequently encouraged and cemented my commitment to her story. This led to my introduction with Lucile Hadžihalilović, and through his endeavors, their development of Earwig into a motion picture.

To Mark Booth's wisdom and insight in the editing of this volume, and his excellent company at our venerable working lunches.

To Karen Geary's brightness and patience, and her team at Hodder & Stoughton.

To my brilliant agent Jon Elek and his team at United Agents.

Constant gratitude to those that gave advice and shared the translation from dyslexic cockney into readable English: Iain Sinclair, Flossie Catling, Sarah Simblet.

For those that were brave enough to read it raw: Tony Grisoni, Roddy Bell, Geoff Cox, Rebecca Hind, Peter Jewkes.

To the memory of Au Metro in Liege, and all the souls that

ever drank, danced and met Satan there. A bar beyond description which inspired the atmosphere in this book.

Love and thanks to the Family Van Der Linden of Puth, who were always there when I found my way back to Limburg.

And again, to Iain and Anna Sinclair for their friendship, humour and endless encouragement.